PLEASE ... WITH SUGAR ON IT

"Mister Tracy, I'd like to hire you for one day," Judith Collins said. "If you don't find out where Thomas is, then I'll call the police."

Trace shook his head. "You don't understand," he said. "You seem to think that I'm some kind of real detective who can find things out like that." He snapped his fingers.

"Then what are you?" she asked.

"I'm a bumbler. I fumble around. I never figure anything out. I just annoy people. I never catch anybody. I'm not a detective. I'm an annoyance clerk. I should work in a department store."

Judith Collins stared at Trace for a long time. Then her shoulders shuddered as if from an explosion deep within a body that Trace suspected was very shapely beneath the shapeless house-dress she wore. She began to sob uncontrollably.

"Please, Mr. Tracy. Please."

Trace sighed. He could never resist good manners.

TRACE
PIGS GET FAT

SIGNET Mysteries You'll Enjoy

TRACE
PIGS GET FAT

WARREN MURPHY

A SIGNET BOOK

NEW AMERICAN LIBRARY

PUBLISHER'S NOTE

This novel is a work of fiction. Names, characters, places, and incidents either are the product of the author's imagination or are used fictitiously, and any resemblance to actual persons, living or dead, events, or locales is entirely coincidental.

NAL BOOKS ARE AVAILABLE AT QUANTITY DISCOUNTS WHEN USED TO PROMOTE PRODUCTS OR SERVICES. FOR INFORMATION PLEASE WRITE TO PREMIUM MARKETING DIVISION, NEW AMERICAN LIBRARY, 1633 BROADWAY, NEW YORK, NEW YORK 10019.

SIGNET TRADEMARK REG. U.S. PAT. OFF. AND FOREIGN COUNTRIES
REGISTERED TRADEMARK—MARCA REGISTRADA
HECHO EN CHICAGO, U.S.A.

SIGNET, SIGNET CLASSIC, MENTOR, PLUME, MERIDIAN AND NAL BOOKS are published by New American Library, 1633 Broadway, New York, New York 10019

First Printing, October, 1985

1 2 3 4 5 6 7 8 9

PRINTED IN THE UNITED STATES OF AMERICA

For Gene and Pat
and Michael and Jessica

1

Sometimes good things happened to good people. That was the way Devlin Tracy felt when he answered the telephone in his Las Vegas condominium apartment and discovered that it was Walter Marks calling.

Usually life demanded that he see Marks in person. On those too-numerous occasions, Tracy not only had to listen to his whiny little voice and see his pinched-up face, but he also had to feel the waves of hatred Marks exuded whenever they had to share the same piece of floor. But today all he had to do was talk to him on the telephone. That was obviously a good thing and Devlin Tracy knew he deserved it because he was obviously a good person.

"Mr. Walter Marks calling," the secretary had said. "Is this Devlin Tracy?"

"None other," Trace said.

"Please hold on for Mr. Marks," she said.

"Certainly," Trace said, and hung up.

He went into the apartment's small kitchen, poured himself a cup of coffee, and found a pack of cigarettes. By the time he brought them back into the living room, the telephone was ringing. Because he had just read an information flier from the telephone company that recommended that a caller ring ten times before hanging up, Trace let it ring nine times before picking up. If Walter Marks' office was not smart enough to read the mail from the telephone company, then they didn't deserve to talk to him.

"Mr. Tracy?" the same secretarial voice grated.

"Yes, indeed. Is this Groucho's secretary?"

"I beg your pardon."

"Never mind. We must have been cut off," Trace said.

She humphed a humph of disbelief. "Please hold on this time," she said coolly.

"I'm waiting right here," Trace said. He didn't have a cigarette lighter. He had cigarettes now but no way to light them.

He hung up again.

The telephone rang while he scoured the apartment for a lighter. He counted the rings as he searched. It was strange—he never seemed able to find a lighter anymore. He decided it was probably because he was spending less time in bars.

Many thought that people who whiled away the hours in taverns were acting out of compulsion. But Trace spent a lot of time in bars because it was the best place to steal a steady supply of disposable cigarette lighters. He started running low on lighters after cutting down on his drinking.

The telephone had rung twelve times when he found a pack of matches in the kitchen. They were printed with the message: "You can be an artist. Draw this face."

Trace would have tried if he could have located a pen, but his pen supply had dwindled along with the cigarette lighter stockpile. Being sober was hell on house supplies.

Eighteen rings.

Trace lit a cigarette.

Nineteen.

He picked up the telephone and said in his most cheerful, have-a-nice-day voice, "Hi! I guess Groucho wants to speak to me?"

"Hold on for Mr. Marks," the secretary replied coldly.

Walter Marks was the vice president for claims of the Garrison Fidelity Insurance Company. Technically, Devlin Tracy worked for him as a free-lance claims investigator. However, both men knew that Trace had his job because he was a friend of Robert Swenson, the president of Garrison Fidelity. This caused Marks a great deal of discomfort because he was a small man, and like many small men, he liked to rule through terror and threats of firing. Since Trace was totally fireproof and impervious to terror, he was not one of Marks' favorites.

"Trace?" came Marks' nastly little voice. He spoke as if there were a penalty for separating his lips.

"Yes, Groucho," Trace said. " 'Tis I."

"What the hell is going on there? Why do you keep hanging up on me?"

"I didn't hang up on you, Walter," Trace said, sipping his coffee, his mind still on that matchbook cover. Draw this face. Maybe he could have some printed up with Walter Marks' picture on them and then the legend: Erase This Face. "I think it's that ditzy secretary of yours. I don't think she knows how to operate the hold button. Anyway, you've got me now. Do you want something or is this just free-form complaining?"

"No. Actually I called to ask you politely to start working off your retainer. Beginning today, Tracy."

"Well, as much as I'd like to, Groucho, I'm afraid I'll have to turn down any assignment you might be planning to stick me with."

"What?"

"It conflicts with previous plans I have made," Trace said.

"What plans?"

"I'm going to San Francisco for a convention."

"There's no insurance convention in San Francisco," Marks said.

"Insurance is just one tiny facet of the gem that is my life," Trace said. "This is a convention of American citizens born in Japan."

"Look Tracy—I know you're Jewish and Irish," Marks said. "How'd you suddenly arrange to be Japanese?"

"Not me. Chico. Her mother is going and we're going to go with her."

"I find it hard to believe that I have to point this out to even a sloth like you but work should come first," Marks said.

"Look at it this way," Trace said. "There's always work, never a shortage of it. But a convention, once missed, is gone forever."

"So is a retainer," Marks snarled. "Then you're turning down the job I've got for you."

"How quick you are on the uptake. Not even the subtlest hint can slide by you unnoticed," Trace said.

"I'll remember this conversation."

"I know. And you'll write it down in your file of reasons to shitcan Devlin Tracy. But just when you think it's worth the effort to try, you'll remember all the millions of dollars I've saved dear old Gone Fishing and you'll change your mind."

"Don't refer to Garrison Fidelity as Gone Fishing," Marks snapped.

"Okay, Groucho."

"And don't call me Groucho."

"Yes, Walter," Trace said.

"I hope the fags attack you in San Francisco," Marks said.

"I'll stay indoors."

"How long will you be gone?"

"Probably ten days," Trace said.

"I'll talk to you when you get back," Marks said.

"I'll count the hours," Trace said.

Trace was dozing on the sofa when the front door to the apartment opened. He opened his eye and mumbled, "Hi, Chico."

"I don't believe it," Michiko Mangini answered. She was tiny and trim with long, lustrous black hair. Her eyes were large, luminous, and dark in the healthy taupe of her face.

Except for a touch of lipstick on her full bow-shaped lips, she wore no makeup. Trace knew she scrubbed it off when she knocked off her shift as a blackjack dealer at the Araby Casino. While she was working, she had to wear a silly-looking harem costume and showgirl makeup, but Chico peeled that persona away as soon as the work shift ended. She was twenty-six but looked younger; she was beautiful but looked better than beautiful. She was also a part-time hooker but they didn't talk about that.

"What don't you believe?" Trace said.

"It's the cocktail hour and you're lying there with a coffee cup in front of you. I thought you'd be shitfaced by now."

"Don't it warm the cockles of your Japanese-Sicilian heart?" Trace said as he swung his feet to the floor and quickly finished the last of the vodka that was in the coffee cup.

Chico was still in the doorway, transferring bags of groceries from the hallway to inside the apartment. Trace thought that her arms always seemed to be filled with groceries. She was lucky that he hardly ate anything; otherwise her shoulders would be thick with muscle and her back permanently swayed from the weight of the load.

"All set for our vacation?" she asked as she started to carry the bags two at a time into the kitchen.

"Yes," he said.

"All packed?"

"No," he said.

"Why not?"

"I knew if I waited long enough you'd do it for me," Trace said.

"Only if you promise that I can leave out that stupid tape recorder," she said.

"Of course leave it out. We're going on vacation, right?"

"Exactly," Chico said. "No secret conversations on tape. No work. Just play for a week."

"Wanna play now?" he asked.

"I'd rather unpack the groceries first," she said.

"Want me to help?"

"No," she said.

"Why not?"

"You always put things in the wrong place. The rice winds up with the spaghetti sauce, the smoked oysters get hidden behind the oatmeal. No, thank you. I'd rather do it myself."

"Actually," Trace said, "I was wondering why you bought groceries at all when we're leaving tomorrow on vacation."

"You never can tell," she said darkly. "Something goes wrong, at least this way we have food to eat."

"I talked to Walter Marks today," Trace said.

"Did he try to ruin our vacation?"

"Of course."

Trace marveled at how efficiently she put things away. The kitchen was only a narrow passageway, sink and refrigerator and range on one side, cabinets and counter on the other, but she always seemed to have room to store the array of bottles, cans, and jars she brought home.

"Food for starving India," he mumbled as he walked by her in the kitchen and rinsed out his coffee cup.

"Why, for the first time in memory, are you washing your own cup?" she asked.

"I want to remove the traces of vodka before you got to it," Trace said.

"You didn't need to. I smelled it as soon as I walked past you."

"Vodka has no smell," Trace said.

"It does."

"What does it smell like?" he asked.

"It has a distinct vodka smell," she said.

"That's nonsense. That's why everybody

drinks vodka, so their wives don't notice it on their breath when they get home. You think all those millions of people are wrong?"

"Wrong as wrong can be," she said. She teetered precariously on a little step stool putting canned goods into the back of a top shelf. "Did you ever hear of any wife anywhere who couldn't tell when her husband had been drinking? Vodka or no vodka, we women always know."

"God, you're insidious," he said.

She turned around and smiled at him. As she stood on the stool, her eyes were almost level with his.

"Remember this," she said, "whenever you get the idea to cheat or mess with me. I always know. I know all." Her eyes sparkled. "You know, maybe it's a sex-related genetic difference? Maybe only men can't smell vodka. All women can. And besides, when you sweat, you excrete it and you smell like a locker room."

"And despite that, you've put up with me all these years," he said. He grabbed her around the waist, spun her off the stool, and kissed her.

"It hasn't been that many years," she said. "Only three."

"Seems like more," he said.

Later that night, Chico packed Trace's clothes for him, with frequent hoots at various garments she found hanging in his closet. As she usually did, she filled a large green Hefty Bag with clothing that she said she absolutely would not ever let him wear again and that she was going to donate to the Volunteers of America clothing drive.

Then she went to sleep.

Trace carefully took all the clothing out of the Hefty Bag and put them back into his closet.

Finally, before going to bed himself, he took the small portable tape recorder and its tiny microphone fashioned in the shape of a golden frog tie clip and hid it in the bottom of his suitcase.

"One never knows, do one?" he mumbled.

2

San Francisco Airport was on its way to being weathered in, so the jetcraft from Las Vegas made swooping lazy circles in the sky for forty-five minutes. Trace made the most of the time by complaining bitterly about not being allowed to smoke or to get a drink.

The stewardess told him huffily, "It's for your own protection, you know."

"We're going to die, aren't we?" Trace said. "We're all going to die."

"Nonsense. Everything is perfectly all right," the stewardess said. She leaned forward and said softly, "And I wish you'd lower your voice. You might alarm the other passengers."

"You think this is alarming them, you just wait until I stand up and start singing 'Nearer My God to Thee.' You'll see alarm."

"You're not allowed to stand up," the stewardess said. "The fasten-seat-belts sign is lit."

"When we plunge into the ocean, can I take off my seat belt?" he asked.

"Madam, is this gentleman with you?" the stewardess asked Chico, who was trying to hide behind a copy of *Mechanix Illustrated*.

"Much as I hate to admit it," Chico said.

"Do you think you could calm him down?"

"Can we do coke?" Trace asked the stewardess. "Coke always calms me down."

Chico dug him in the ribs with her elbow. "I'll try to restrain him," she told the attendant.

The stewardess nodded and walked away and Chico snarled at Trace, "Why do you say things like that? You never did coke in your life."

"Because I like to keep these people on their toes," he said. "They're flying serious cargo. Me. She's a lightweight, Chico, a lightweight. Stewardi all used to be nurses, and then they were all *Playboy* bunnies or something, and now they're all goddamn file clerks. They don't make stews like they used to."

"Actually, neither do you," Chico said.

"A lot you know," Trace said. "And why wouldn't she give me my pair of wings when I finished all my peanuts?"

"Trace, she told you she was out of wings. You've got a hundred pairs of plastic wings home from every airline."

"I always get wings," he grumbled, and slumped down in his seat.

When they left the plane, the stewardess was waiting at the cabin door wishing everyone a nice day. Chico said, "Thank you." Trace said, "Lightweight."

They were almost an hour late touching down and they found Chico's mother sitting disconsolately near the baggage carousel.

The tiny Japanese woman was wearing a blue pantsuit. Her name was Nobuko but everyone called her Emmie, which Trace could never understand. The resemblance between the woman and her daughter was striking, but the older woman seemed much more delicate. Chico's late father was an Italian sailor, and the combination of his genes with her mother's had given Chico a more healthy look than her mother had. The older woman looked as if she should have her face powdered white and be standing stock-still on a stage somewhere; Chico looked as if she should be sweating her way through a difficult ballet.

"Hi, Mom. Sorry we're late," Chico said.

"Hello, Michiko. Hello, You." From the first time she had met Trace, she had addressed him as You, since she thought that both his names—Devlin and Tracy—were basically unpronounceable.

"The Widow Mangini," Trace said, leaning over to kiss her forehead.

"Why the long face?" Chico asked.

"I thought you not come. I thought I kill myself if you not come," Emmie said.

"Bad weather. The plane was slow landing," Chico said.

"We did almost die," Trace said. "I thought the plane was going to crash."

"My fault plane almost crash, you come to

see me. If plane crash, I kill myself," Chico's mother said.

The luggage carousel was empty.

"Your luggage must be in the office," Trace told Emmie. "I'll get it."

"It brew."

Trace looked at Chico.

"Blue," she explained.

Trace nodded and asked the woman, "You have one suitcase?"

"No. I have two suits-case."

"Two suits-case coming up," Trace said. He left the two women talking in Japanese and found the luggage in the baggage handling office.

A storm was gathering as they rode, three to a cab seat, into San Francisco. The wind seemed to pick up in intensity as they passed Candlestick Park, the baseball stadium a few miles outside the heart of the city, and Trace wondered what kind of genius had decided to build a baseball stadium there.

He had seen the Giants play there once years before. A batter had swung under a ball and hit a high pop fly to the infield. The infielders had all moved in toward the pitcher's mound to catch the pop-up, and then the wind took over. When the ball came down, it was on the other side of the left-field fence for a home run.

Playing baseball there was like playing Ping-Pong in an open field on a windy day. The weather was always a tenth man, but it was a lunatic tenth and one never knew which side he was playing on at any given moment.

"What that big thing, You?" Trace's mother asked, pointing to the stadium.

"Candlestick Park," he said.

"If park, where trees?"

"It stadium," Trace said. "Where they play *beisboru*." When he was with Emmie, he found himself talking in pigeon English with his four words of Japanese thrown in. It was not condescension, but an honest effort to make his speech simple so she could understand.

"Oh, yes. *Beisboru*," Emmie said. "I like *beisboru*. Hot dogs, fat undertakers, beer commercials."

Trace looked at Chico again. "Don't tell me, umpires, right?"

"Blue suits. Fat undertakers, right," Chico said.

"I loot for Pittsburgh Pilots," Emmie said.

"God, I ruv you," Trace said.

"I ruv you too, You."

"Should I reave?" Chico asked.

Their hotel was a new modern structure on the fringe of San Francisco's compact and clean Chinatown. Trace stayed with the luggage to make sure the bellhop didn't steal anything while Chico checked them all in.

A large red-and-white sign across the lobby read WELCOME, JAPANESE-AMERICAN GUESTS, and then presumably repeated the same message in Oriental characters beneath the large English letters.

"I got us adjoining rooms," Chico said softly to Trace as they waited for the elevator.

"Is that wise?" Trace said.

"Why not?"

"Well, if your mother's staying right next door to us, what about your little squeals of ecstasy? Don't you have any modesty?"

"It's been so long since I had a little squeal of ecstasy that I didn't even make it a factor in my planning," Chico said.

"There's always a first time," Trace said.

"Actually, I had sort of a different arrangement in mind," Chico said.

"Namely?"

"Here's the elevator," she said.

As soon as the door slid open on the third floor, Trace knew with an alarming clarity what arrangement Chico had in mind. She was staying in a double room with her mother. Trace was in the single room adjoining theirs. Chico came into unpack his suitcase.

"This is suckful," Trace said. "I hate this already."

"I can't just stay in your room. Not when we're traveling with my mother."

"Why not? She knows we live together in Las Vegas."

"That's different. She's not *in* Las Vegas."

"You mean if she lived in Las Vegas, you and I wouldn't live together?"

"Not without benefit of clergy. I'd live with her," Chico said.

"That is one fine how-the-hell-do-you-do," Trace said.

"Leave your door unlocked; I'll try to sneak in some night," Chico said.

"Knock first. I might be entertaining guests," Trace said sullenly.

"What ho! Smelling strangeness. What's this?" Chico said. She held up Trace's small tape recorder, which she had just ferreted out of the bottom of his suitcase.

"It looks like my tape recorder. How'd that get there? I thought you weren't going to pack it."

"Don't lie to me, you goddamn barbarian. Why'd you bring this thing?"

"I confess. I don't know why. I just always feel better when it's around," Trace said.

"That's the first strike against our vacation, having this thing around," she said.

"You know I told Groucho no, I'm not working. You know that. I don't know why, I just brought it." He tried to smile, but her departing back did not seem to notice.

A few minutes later, Emmie came into Trace's room through the connecting door, just as he was turning on the television.

"How you like your loom?" she asked.

"I like yours better," Trace said.

"You want switch looms? I stay here, you stay with Michiko?"

"She wouldn't do that," Trace said.

"She dumb sometime. You two live together. You. Why not you stay together on vacation?"

"I know what you're up to," Trace said. "You want this room so when you pick up strange men, you'll have a place to bring them to without Chico seeing you."

"Very funny, You. But not bad idea," she said.

"Well, I'm not helping you become a fallen woman. Get back in your own room," Trace said.

"Okay. Just asking," she said.

She went back into the other room and Trace heard her tell Chico, "He said he not want to stay with you."

"Why not?" Chico asked.

"He say if I stay alone, I fall down," Emmie said.

"I said 'fallen woman,' " Trace shouted.

"Right. Fall down," said Emmie.

Trace closed the door between the rooms with a sigh.

For this vacation and this vacation alone, Chico had lifted the restrictions on Trace's drinking, so he had room service send up two bottles of vodka.

He was lying on his bed, drinking and watching a *Ben Casey* rerun on television. He decided that if he were ever really sick, he wanted a doctor just like Ben Casey. The hell with his being nasty; at least he was trying to keep patients alive. Doctor Kildare was good for upset stomachs; Marcus Welby might keep you alive through a cold, but if he got really sick, send out the call for Butcher Ben. "Screw hospital rules, Dr. Zorba. You go draw diagrams on your blackboard and let me save this degenerate's life."

The telephone rang.

"Mr. Tracy?" The woman's voice was vaguely familiar.

"Yes."

"Hold on, please, for Walter Marks."

The call took Trace so much by surprise that he didn't have time to hang up before Marks was on the phone.

"Trace. I'm glad I found you."

"How'd you track me down? You didn't tell my ex-wife and the two savages where I am, did you?"

"No. And I won't either," said Marks with unaccustomed warmth.

"You're up to something," Trace said. "How'd you find me?"

"A hunch. I had my secretary check all the hotels near Chinatown."

"That's a lot of work to go to just to ruin my vacation," Trace said.

"This is important," Marks said. "Listen, Trace, I'd like you to do me a favor."

"I can't believe my ears. You're asking me for a favor?"

"That's right."

"If I weren't lying down already, I'd have to sit down," Trace said.

"Take it anyway you want," Marks said.

"I know how hard this must be for you."

"I have a friend in San Francisco," Marks said.

"And you want me to kill him so your no-friend record can be unblemished again?" Trace said.

"No. I just want you to talk to him."

"He's your friend?" Trace said.

"Yes."

"Then what would we possibly have to talk about?"

"This fella needs some advice," Marks said.

"You're willing to have me give him advice? He must be some friend," Trace said.

"He is. We were in school together."

"What's he do? What kind of advice?"

"He's an insurance man with us," Marks said. "He thinks he might have a problem with a policy."

"I don't know anything about insurance," Trace said.

"But you know something about missing people and policework. This might be a police problem. You see, he just wrote a big insurance policy on some guy and now the guy seems to be missing."

"The cops looking for him?"

"No, not yet," Marks said. "That's what he wants advice about."

"I don't know. I'm here on vacation," Trace said.

"How long can it take you? I'm asking you as a favor. Talk to Mike."

"Mike?"

"Michael Mabley. That's the name of his agency," Marks said.

"I don't know."

There was a long silence over the telephone. Finally, Marks said, "Please."

"Please?" Trace said.

"Please."

"What's his number?" Trace said.

3

They were at the convention welcoming dinner, sitting at a table of ten, surrounded by another five hundred people clustered around other tables of ten. The sign over the dais said it was the fortieth anniversary of the Japanese-American Unity Association. Trace figured that the organization had been founded in 1945, the same year Japan surrendered to end World War II. Most likely, Trace thought, it had started the day after the surrender.

"Look, there's one," he said to Chico. "And there's another." He pointed across the room.

"One what?" she said.

"A Jap without a camera," he said. "There's another. Whoever said all Japanese carried cameras?"

"Easy on the Jap stuff," Chico said. "These people will sliver you into sushi."

"That's another thing. This rooms smells like raw fish," Trace said.

"And white people smell like kielbasa," Chico said. "Why are you so grouchy anyway?"

"I didn't think everyone was going to speak Japanese," Trace said. "I don't speak Japanese."

"What'd you think they were going to speak at a Japanese convention?" she asked.

"English, dammit. We're in America. Well, San Francisco anyway."

"Go with the flow," Chico said. "Try to blend in with the natives."

"How can I blend in with the natives when I'm fifteen inches taller than the next biggest native?"

"Make friends. The guy next to you looks nice," Chico said.

Trace looked at the elderly Japanese man next to him. He wore a nametag that read, MISTER NISHIMOTO. No first name. Under it were Japanese kangi characters. The man was staring at his plate of colorless salad, seemingly absorbed.

"Looks like fun," Trace said. "If we get to be real good friends, maybe someday I could just call him Mister."

"Very funny," Chico said. "It was a lot funnier than your writing Dev-rin Tlacy on your nametag."

"I wanted to blend in. I didn't think it was going to be like this. I feel like a hairy savage sitting here." On the other side of Chico, her mother was talking high speed to a Japanese woman, and Trace said, "What are they talking about? I bet they're talking about me."

"My mother is telling everyone that you're Ainu, one of the poor Japanese whites."

"I know what Ainu is," Trace said.

"Why are you just picking at your food?" Chico asked.

"I always pick at my food. It's goddamn octopus. I'm lucky it isn't picking at me."

"It's not octopus; it's squid. Eat. It's good for you."

"I don't want to eat," Trace said. "This is the most rotten vacation I was ever on. This is worse than my honeymoon with the Hulkster."

"We just got here," Chico said placidly. "We haven't had enough time yet to make it rotten. Is something bothering you?"

"I thought we'd spend some time together. We're not going to spend any time together. All of you are going to be down here talking about the Battle of Midway. I'm about as welcome as a survivor from the Bataan Death March."

"Bataan," the man next to him said aloud. His face broke into a big smile. "You in Bataan too?"

"Yes," Trace lied.

"I too. I not see you."

"I spent most of my time hiding in a ditch."

"Sorry I missed you," Mr. Nishimoto said. He smiled again.

"Don't you think he knows I was too young for World War Two?" Trace asked Chico softly.

"No. All you whites look alike to us," Chico said.

"Us?" Trace said.

"Us. *Adiós*, kemo-sabe," Chico said.

"Go ahead. Spend your time with your mother," Trace said. He pushed his salad around the plate with his fork. He had insisted upon a fork even though everyone else was eating with chopsticks.

"Try saving a few minutes for me," Trace said.

"What a baby you are. After Momma goes to bed tonight, you and I will sneak out," Chico said.

"I don't want to go *out*," Trace said.

Chico's mother leaned across to speak to him. She put her hand on his wrist.

"You?" Emmie said.

"Yes?"

"Have good time?" she asked.

"Wonderful," Trace said.

"Good. I have good time too. These people all Japanese," she said as if he might not have noticed.

Trace got up to leave between the raw fish and the speeches.

"I'm going to the bar," he told Chico.

"They're opening a bar here. You don't have to go," she said.

"I don't want to drink rice wine," he said.

"Be civilized, though. Don't drink like a lunatic," she said.

"See you later," he said.

"Try *oyasumi nasai*. That means good night," Chico said.

"Try *sayonara*," Trace said. "That means good-bye forever."

Mr. Nishimoto's face brightened again. "Oh?" he said, looking at Trace. "*Sayonara. Sayonara.*" And before Trace had fully vacated it, he was sliding into Trace's seat next to Chico.

Trace growled and left.

One of the worst things about changing your drinking habits, Trace had decided, was that the changes could become a new habit, just as imperious as the last.

For years he had drunk only vodka, vodka from Finland, vodka by the tubful. And then, in a flurry of guilt, remorse, and henpecking, he had switched to wine to please Chico, who was worried that someday his liver might explode.

That had been months ago and now he had gotten used to wine. But Trace never got used to the looks bartenders gave him when he ordered it without thinking. They regarded wine drinkers differently from how they regarded vodka drinkers.

"They think I'm a wimp," he told Chico.

"Who cares what bartenders think?" Chico had said.

"I do," he said. "Bartenders are my only friends."

"That's all changing now," she had said.

"And once you sober up, more people will like you. New vistas will open for you. You'll rub shoulders with people who have a first language."

If he expected a curious look when he walked into the hotel bar and asked for a carafe, he could have forgotten it. This was San Francisco, and the bartender looked like the kind who poured wine drinks all day long. He wore a headband, earrings in both ears, and had tattoos on the backs of his hands. A key ring jangled at his belt.

"Red or white, sir?" he asked. God, yes, he lisped.

"Vodka," Trace said. "Finlandia."

When he settled down with the drink, he had the bartender bring him a telephone and he dialed Michael Mabley's number.

The phone rang three times and a tape-recording clicked in.

"Hello, this is the phone number of Michael Mabley and the Michael Mabley Insurance Agency. Even insurance men need some time off, and since this is the weekend, none of us is available. But if you'll leave your name and number and a brief message, we'll get back to you as soon as we can. Our regular office hours, which are the best time to call, are nine to five, Monday through Friday, and nine till noon on Saturday. Speak at the signal."

Trace waited for the beep and said, "My name is Devlin Tracy and I wanted to buy a ten-million-dollar life-insurance policy. I'd like

to do business with you, but since I've offended you by calling on a Sunday night, I
apologize and I'll call another agency. However, if you decide you would like to handle
this matter on this weekend day, you can try
to reach me at . . ." Trace read the hotel telephone number and extension off the instru-
ment, then hung up.

The bartender reached for the telephone,
but Trace held up his hand.

"I'm expecting a call back in a moment,"
he said. "Fill it again please."

Before the glass was topped, the telephone
was ringing. The bartender answered, then
said, "Your name Tracy?"

Trace nodded and took the phone.

Michael Mabley spoke fast, as if he was
worried about being interrupted.

"Mr. Tracy, this is Michael Mabley. I got
your message about the insurance policy. Sorry
I couldn't pick up the telephone right away,
but I was working with a client. I don't like to
get on the phone when I'm with a client 'cause
I like to give them my undivided attention.
That's the way we operate here at the Mabley
agency. Every client is number one in our
book. Número Uno. That's the way this agency's been built and that's why we're the 287th
largest agency in California, not counting car-
insurance agencies." He finally paused for
breath and Trace said, "Very commendable."

"You said something on the telephone about
a policy?" Mabley said.

"Yes, but that was a lie," Trace said.

"I beg your pardon?"

"That was a lie. I just wanted to get your attention," Trace said. "I'm Devlin Tracy Doesn't that mean anything to you?"

"No. Should it?"

"I'm with Garrison Fidelity. Marks asked me to call you."

"Oh. You're the investigator he mentioned."

"What did he say about me?" Trace asked.

"He said you worked for them sometimes."

"Did he seem pleased with my work?"

"He sort of said that you had a personality problem, actually," Mabley said. "Nothing serious, mind you. Just that you were difficult to get along with sometimes."

"Good," Trace said. "That's the way I always want Groucho to think of me. He said you had a problem."

"Groucho. That's a hot one. Is that his nickname?"

"No. Actually Walter is his nickname," Trace said. "His real name is Groucho, but he doesn't like to use it because . . . well, you know the insurance business. People are pretty conservative. They might not feel right handing their money to somebody named Groucho Marks. But he really loves the name. It was a favorite of his father, Karl, too. Next time you talk to him, tell him I told you. So what's your problem?"

"I don't think it's a real big problem," Mabley said. He had the voice of a natural insurance man, Trace thought. It treaded through life's waters, never judgmental, never anything but monotone. It was a voice without a bone in it. He was saying, "Just a problem about procedure, but I don't know what's the best thing to do. That's why I called Walter."

"Groucho. Remember. Groucho," Trace said.

"Right. I've got to remember that. Groucho Marks. That's a good one."

"So what's the problem?" Trace repeated.

"Listen, could I see you tomorrow? It's too complicated maybe to go into on the telephone."

"That's kind of a pain in the ass," Trace said. "You see, I'm at this real swinging convention and I'd hate to miss a moment of it."

"I'm in the city," Mabley said. "I could meet you. I'll buy you lunch."

"Your restaurant doesn't serve octopus, does it?" Trace asked.

"I don't think so. I could probably get them to get some for you, though, if it's real important."

"No, no," Trace said. "Just leave things the way they are. I'll come down tomorrow. Around noontime."

"Good. I'll be waiting for you." Mabley gave Trace an address in San Francisco's rundown Mission District and said, "You can't miss it. There's a big sign of a hand over the front door."

"Open, no doubt," Trace said.

"That's a hot one," Mabley said, and Trace hung up.

He had many drinks more while waiting for Chico. She never did come into the bar. When he went up to his room just after "last call," he listened at the adjoining door. Trace could hear two sets of little Japanese snores, mother and daughter, and he went to bed annoyed and frustrated.

First, though, he took a piece of hotel stationery, wrote a note, and slid it under the door.

It read: "Chico, Please don't disturb us. We'll probably sleep late."

In the morning he found a note under his side of the door: "Dear Trace, The four of us didn't see your note until this morning. Hope we didn't make too much noise. Love, Bob and Chico and Ted and Emmie."

4

It was going to be a fun day at the convention. That was for sure. Trace met Chico and her mother emerging from the hotel's coffee shop, and Chico went back inside with him to have another breakfast. She gave him a complete rundown on the convention schedule.

First there was going to be a lecture on Japanese industry and its place in a changing world. In Japanese. And then there was going to be a lecture on Japanese film and its place in a changing world. Then they were going to show a film, *Seven Brides for Seven Samurai*, in Japanese.

Then they were going to a lunchtime lecture on Japan's cuisine and its place in a changing world, in an effort to find out what they had eaten for lunch.

"That's easy," Trace said. "Say octopus if they ask questions."

Trace ordered a half-piece of toast and coffee. Chico ordered something called the Fisherman's Breakfast, which included pancakes, eggs, and fried oysters, among other things.

"I thought you just ate," Trace said.

"I did. But I had the Cable Car Special Breakfast and I was wondering what was in this one," she said. Her mouth full of Trace's toast, she said, "I think the way you close your mind to other cultures is the mark of a small person."

"You mean all this Japanese culture around here?" he asked, and she nodded. "Well, that's how little you know," he said. "I happen to like other cultures very much. Greek, French, English, I am very big on all those cultures."

"You wish," she said.

"Are you really going to all these lectures?"

"Mama-san says we go, we go. You don't have to," Chico said.

"And what do I do?"

"Wander the streets," she said. "Borrow one of my mother's cameras. She's still got the six you gave her. Take pictures of the local flora and fauna and fagola."

"I just may buckle on my tape recorder and go do some work," he said.

"I'm sure you may," she said. She returned a quarter-slice of toast to his plate and bent down over her own breakfast.

Back in his room, Trace taped the small tape recorder to his right side. A long wire plugged into the microphone jack and he threaded the wire under his shirt and through a buttonhole and attached it to the tie clip shaped like a golden frog. The gold mesh that covered the frog's mouth was the cover for a very strong microphone.

Trace checked that the machine was working, put an extra tape into his jacket pocket, and left the hotel.

It was cool and cloudy—good weather for San Francisco—so Trace decided to walk to Michael Mabley's office.

Walking along, Trace decided that it wasn't that he disliked California. The fact was that he didn't understand it. The state was certainly physically beautiful. Everything God had managed to cram into the world had a counterpart in California, from desert to mountain, from prairies to forest.

But the state had no discernible soul. It reminded Trace of a Christmas package. The box was beautiful and decorated with gold and silver; and inside, there was a layer of beautiful wrapping paper, and then another layer of wrapping paper more beautiful than the first. But no matter how long you dug or how deeply you rooted around inside the box, you never found anything more than beautiful wrapping paper. No soul.

New York had its nasty busy-ness and Chicago had its feel of muscled corruption. Even New Hampshire looked nice, but underneath was the knowledge that everybody in the state would steal the pennies from a dead man's eyes.

But California had no feel, and neither did

Californians. There was a quintessential New York and Alabaman and Texan, but no quintessential Californian.

Unless it was a movie producer. They were perhaps the only indigenous California creatures that could not be transplanted elsewhere and feel right at home.

What an epitaph for a state: "It gave us the movie producer."

He amended that fifteen minutes later when he met Michael Mabley. California spawned both movie producers and people who wanted to look like movie producers.

Mabley wore a white-on-white silk shirt, open at the throat, with enough chains around his neck to make Mr. T look like Mahatma Gandhi. He was a little soft around the belly and his hair was frizz-curled with a permanent wave to make it look less thin. His French cuffs held large golden helmet cuff links that looked like a promotional giveaway from Caesar's Palace, and he wore red suspenders. His lips were almost invisible, his mouth just a slit in the Pillsbury Doughboy puff that was his fleshy face. His eyes were dark and looked watery. The creases in his pants were so sharp they could have cut steak, and he wore a large golden-buckled cowboy-style belt.

Trace got the feeling he would know the year-to-date gross of every film made in Hollywood so far this year.

He pumped Trace's hand inside his office

and said, "How are you, Mr. Tracy? Hot enough for you?"

"It's not warm at all," Trace said.

"I know," Mabley said with a smile that visited his mouth for only a millisecond before vanishing. "I always say that. Sort of like a trademark."

"Oh, I got it. Like the suspenders and the gold chains and the cowboy belt."

"Right. Exactly. Something like that makes it easier for people to remember you," Mabley said.

"Asking people if it's hot enough when the weather's freezing will probably get them to remember you too," Trace said.

"Sure," Mabley said agreeably. Another quick smile vanished without a trace of its ever having been there. "You up for lunch?"

"That's another good one," Trace said. "Up for lunch. Sure. I'm up for lunch. I'll take a lunch with you."

"Then we ought to get this show—"

"On the road?" Trace said.

"Right, as rain. Wait, I'll get my jacket," Mabley said.

He walked to the back and Trace looked at the pictures on the wall behind Mabley's desk. There was one of the agent surrounded by twenty blond young boys, doomed to grow up to be surfers, under a banner that read: "MABLEY'S MAULERS, LITTLE LEAGUE CHAMPIONS." There was a picture of Mabley shaking hands with someone who must have been a California politician because he managed to look both healthy and corrupt at the same time. There was a citation from the press office of the Insurance Institute of America, giving Mabley the coveted Needham Award for excellence in public relations, and another citation from the Bay Area Artisans' Craft Guild thanking him for his generous financial sponsorship and his service as a director.

At least there wasn't a picture of him shaking hands with Richard Nixon, Trace thought.

Mabley came back inside wearing a red plaid jacket that looked as if it had been won in a crap game with a horse.

Based on that garment, Trace expected a restaurant with balloons hanging from the ceiling and a go-go girl dancing on the bar, but the restaurant, only two blocks away, turned out to be wood-paneled and not brightly lit. They had a table in a far corner away from the kitchen and the customer traffic.

Their waitress was a cute blonde wearing improbably high-heeled shoes and with improbably beautiful legs. She was chewing gum.

She called Mabley "Señor Mabley" and he chuckled and ordered "my usual." Mabley looked at Trace knowingly.

Trace said, "I'll have my usual too."

"What's your usual, pardner?" she said.

"Do you have anything with an umbrella in it?"

She bellowed over her shoulder. "Hey, Charlie, we got any drinks with umbrellas in them?"

"No," came the return bellow.

"No," she told Trace.

"Finlandia vodka. Rocks," he said.

"Very good," she said.

As she walked away, Mabley said, "Nice legs, huh?"

"Pretty good," Trace admitted. True was true.

"All the girls in here are knockouts. That's why I come here." He leered at Trace and rolled his eyes.

"Well, that one sure seems to know you," Trace said.

"Yeah. They know me. And I know them. Bachelor's paradise. I bring my dinner dates here too. Impresses the waitresses."

This person deserved to be Walter Marks' friend. He was a nasty, crass, little man just like Walter Marks. They were two peas from the same pod. Mabley might be a bigger pea, but then everybody was bigger than Walter Marks.

Trace wanted lunch to be over. He wanted to get out of there. But he didn't want to go back to a Japanese convention. Maybe he would go to a movie. He hadn't seen a movie since *Deep Throat*, and he had fallen asleep during that one before anything happened.

He wished Chico were there so she could see how he had carefully not called the waitress "honey" or "sweetheart." Chico said he only did this because he was a sexist and didn't understand how offensive it was to women. Trace said it was no more offensive than calling a man you didn't know "chief" or "pal."

She said he didn't understand. He said he would never understand if she didn't explain.

"It's nothing like pal or chief," she had said. "That's an expression of equality. Sweetheart or honey is an expression of condescension and it's patronizing. You're immediately putting yourself in a position of superiority over the woman. A—because you don't even have to bother to learn her name; and B—because you're assuming intimacy as a given on your terms and she has no voice in the matter. This, Trace, is a fact, and you are insensitive not to understand it."

"You've been reading the Spenser books again," Trace had said. "You sound like Susan Silverman."

"That is immaterial."

"How, then, does one address a waitress, for instance, whose name one does not know but who seems nice and deserves to be called something more than waitress?"

"Try miss. Or ma'am if she is one of the few people in the world older than you are," Chico had said.

"Not mizz?" Trace had asked.

"No, not mizz. Mizz always precedes a name. It never stands alone as a form of address."

"God, just what I needed, a Japanese-Sicilian who's not only treacherous but pendantic too," Trace had said.

"And correct. Don't forget correct," Chico had said.

When the waitress came back with their drinks, Mabley said, "Thanks, darling." His drink was pink and foamy.

Trace said, "Should I call you miss or ma'am?"

"Honey will do," she said.

"I thought women didn't like being called honey or dear or sweetheart."

"I don't mind. Honey's my name."

"Honey? Really?"

"Really," she said. "Now don't say that's sweet. Please don't."

"I wasn't going to say that at all," said Trace, who had been planning to say that exact thing. "I was merely going to ask you what your last name was. Does it start with a B?"

"Very funny, Honey B, I've heard it before. The name's Johnson."

"Thank you," Trace said. When she left, he sipped his drink and asked Mabley, "What's this all about?" He clicked on his tape recorder.

"I thought you'd never ask," Mabley said.

"Another thing you always say?"

"No, I'm serious. When you didn't want to talk in the car coming over here, I. . . ."

Trace shook his head. Something had seemed wrong about the restaurant and now he knew what it was. He couldn't smell garlic in the air. Any restaurant that didn't smell of garlic was not to be trusted. This one especially because it smelled of fresh air. He looked around, suspecting that they had ionizers on, hidden in the room, to give everybody a thunderstorm high. What the hell, it was California.

"No," he said to Mabley. "I didn't want to talk in the car 'cause I don't like to talk in cars. At least, not business. You just get to a good part and all of a sudden some lunatic with M.D. license plates comes racing out of a sidestreet and if you escape with your life, you've got to start all over again. So now we're here and we can talk."

"Love the way you do business, baby," Mabley said.

"I'm thrilled," Trace said.

"Anyway, about two weeks ago, this guy and his wife called me to get an insurance policy."

"Who are they?" Trace asked.

"His name is Thomas Collins and his wife is Judith. So they come to the office and they want an insurance policy on Collins' life."

"How big?"

"Two hundred thousand," Mabley said. He waited for a moment until Trace nodded. "So we went through all the routine stuff, zip, zip, zip, and got the policy. Then last Friday, the finished policy came into the office, so I drove over to their house to deliver it. I talked to the wife, and you know, Tracy, there was like something funny going on."

"Like what?"

"I didn't know, I couldn't put my finger on it, but there was something. So I talked to the wife awhile and then it turns out that her husband is missing."

"How missing? There's all kinds of missing," Trace said.

"He had been gone for three days and she hadn't seen or heard from him. She was all teary about this, you know, and it took me a long time to get it out of her. I think she was glad to have somebody to tell."

"I think the police would have been the somebody she should tell," Trace said. "Why bother telling you?"

"I mentioned that. I said, tell the police. You never saw a woman so scared."

"Why's she afraid of the police?" Trace asked.

"Not the police. She's scared of her husband. I guess he's some kind of tyrant or something because, well, I finally figured it out, what it was is that she was afraid to talk to the cops: if she did and then her husband came home, he'd be mad because she embarrassed him. I wouldn't put it past him that he's some kind of wife-beater or something because she was scared to death of making him mad."

"She still hasn't heard from him?"

"No. I called her this morning before I came to the office to meet you. Still no word and now it's been five days. But she still hasn't called the cops in."

"Still afraid?" Trace asked, and Mabley nodded. "The husband ever turn up missing before?" Trace asked. "A lot of guys get lost a lot without checking in with their wives, and then they come back, just like before."

"No. She said he travels sometimes for a few days, but if he's going to be away, he always calls. That's what she said anyway."

"She should call the cops," Trace said.

"That's what I told her."

"What I don't understand is how any of this involves you. Or Gone Fishing, for that matter."

"Gone Fishing?"

"Garrison Fidelity," Trace said.

"Oh. The insurance company. That's a good one. Well, anyway, I didn't know what I should do. Maybe I should call the cops or maybe I should butt out. But two hundred thousand is a lot of money. Anyway, the policy was so fresh I didn't want anyone to think I was a patsy for some kind of scam. That's when I called Walter."

"Groucho," Trace corrected.

"Sorry. Groucho. So I was just kind of looking for guidance. You know, I don't want to be the cause of having Judith Collins get the whap whaled out of her by her husband either."

"How did my name come up?" Trace asked.

"Wal—Groucho said that maybe an investigator should take a look at it, just in case there was some kind of fraud involved. He said there's a lot of 'Quick-policy/accidental-suicide' going around.''

"Groucho's suspicious," Trace said. "He thinks Indira Gandhi was an insurance fraud."

"So he told me maybe he'd send out an investigator and then he called and told me you were in the area and it was lucky because you were Garrison's best man and he'd ask you to stop in."

"He said I was their best man?" Trace asked.

"That's what he said. And I can see how he'd think that," Mabley said.

"Why?"

"Because you seem to be right on the ball. Like a guy knows the score and how to get things done," the insurance agent said.

"Skip all that, it's making me sick. Tell me about this Collins. What's he do anyway?"

"He's a real-estate man. It's a pretty big firm around here, Collins and Rose. I was surprised that Collins didn't have any insurance before this."

"How old is he?" Trace asked.

"Maybe forty-five or so. Your age. Forties. It's on the application."

"Forties?" Trace said. "My age? I'm just forty. Just barely. Only seven months ago was my birthday. I'm so fresh at forty I still think of myself in the thirties."

"Well, you don't look it," Mabley said.

"And I hate your stupid jacket," Trace said.

"No, no," Mabley said. "It's not that you look old. It's just that you're a big investigator and all, and you couldn't have that much experience and still be so young, you know." He seemed happy with that excuse, so he repeated it. "I didn't think you could be so experienced and young too."

"Yeah, okay," Trace said. "This real-estate firm, you say it's doing well?"

"It's hard for a real-estate company not to do well in California," Mabley said. "I think I should've gone into real estate instead of insurance. God isn't making anymore real estate, you know. Especially around here."

"Who is Rose?"

"Collins' partner. I never met him."

"Okay. What do you know about the Collinses?" Trace asked.

Mabley shrugged. "Nothing really. I mean, I met them when they came in for insurance that Saturday morning, but that's about it. I talked to her since then, when the policy came, is all."

"That's another thing. Why'd you deliver the policy to them? Don't you just mail it?"

"I figured with all Collins' real-estate deals, it might be good advertising to deliver the policy personally. Every real-estate deal needs title insurance and stuff like that, and I figured maybe I could get a foot in the door," Mabley said.

He finished his drink, wiped the pink froth off his lips, and looked Trace in the eyes. Trace didn't like his eyes. They looked like the eyes of a whiny dog.

"So can you help me?" Mabley asked.

"What help do you need?"

"I don't know. I thought maybe I missed something. Maybe I should have forced the wife to go to the police. Maybe you could talk to her."

"I hate to talk to wives," Trace said. "You already did the right thing by calling Groucho. At least he knows you're not trying to skin the company."

"Should I call the police?"

"I don't think it's any of your business," Trace said.

"Don't you think Mrs. Collins should call the police?"

"And that's none of my business," Trace said. "Things should just be left alone. They'll sort themselves out in time. They always do."

"I don't know," Mabley said. "I'm kind of surprised with you. I expected—"

"Expected what?" Trace said.

"Somehow, I don't know. I expected you to go see Judith and tell her to call the police or find out she's lying or something, and then the whole matter would be cleared up."

"You think she's lying?"

Mabley shook his head. "No. If you meet her, you'd see. Just a sweet little woman. Butter wouldn't melt in her mouth. Why don't you go see her?"

"I'm on vacation," Trace said.

"It'd only take you a few minutes."

Trace thought about the afternoon convention program and Octopus, Its Gastronomic Role in a Changing World, and said, "Give me her address."

When they left the restaurant, it had started to rain.

"You walked, didn't you?" Mabley asked.

"Yeah."

"I'll drive you back to your hotel."

Mabley's car was a doctor-sized gray Lincoln with more electronic equipment than most houses. Trace had ignored it on the way to the restaurant but now he hated it.

"Car by Radio Shack," Trace mumbled as he picked up a pair of galoshes encrusted with dried red mud from the front floor and put them in the back.

"I didn't know people still wore galoshes," Trace said. He remembered being forced to wear them as a child; it had never occurred to him that an adult might put them on voluntarily.

"Got to protect Mr. Gucci," Mabley said, pointing toward his patent-leather loafers. "I had to change a tire."

That settled it, Trace decided. No more chances for Michael Mabley. The galoshes were bad enough, but any man who'd wear patent-leather loafers with someone else's initials on them was no friend of his. Walter Marks could have him.

But a deal was a deal and he was going to talk to Mrs. Collins, before Gone Fishing had to shell out a couple of hundred grand. He figured he'd give her ten minutes. After all, Walter Marks had said "please" to him.

5

The Collins home was at the end of one of those dead-ended streets that gets called a court. The roadway is concluded with a circle, around which houses are packed with just enough room beside them for a driveway with car.

It was an arrangement, Trace thought, that benefited nobody but the builder, who was able to jam more houses into less space. On second thought, maybe it also benefited people who wanted to have an address on a court.

In the middle of the circled roadway was a dot of grass big enough for a flagpole. The pole was there, but no flag, which didn't surprise Trace. Probably all these California types couldn't agree on what kind of flag to put up now that there were flags for whales and poetry and marihuana legalization. Perish forbid that anyone should think of putting up an American flag.

Trace walked past an early-70's Plymouth

Duster parked in the driveway and rang the doorbell of the Collins home.

Judith Collins was 90 percent of the way toward being a beauty, and Trace had never before realized just how important the other 10 percent was.

She had natural red hair, but she wore it wrong. It hung limp and lifeless around her face, without curl or wave, and Trace had always felt that red hair should be blowsy and breezy to look natural. Redheads were made by God to look as if they had just crawled out from under the sheets with a football team. Mrs. Collins' mouth was full, but she wore no lipstick and so her lips just seemed to fade into her face. Her nose was turned-up pert and her eyes large and green, but they were just there. A little makeup would have made them worth traveling to see. If ever a woman were a candidate for one of those beauty magazine make-overs, it was Judith Collins.

Trace put her age in the last thirties. About the same age as his. Screw Michael Mabley.

The women kept the screen door closed when she opened the front door.

"Yes?" she said.

"Mrs. Collins?"

"Yes."

"My name is Tracy. Mike Mabley suggested I talk to you."

"Mike Mabley?"

"The insurance man who wrote the policy for your husband. I'm with his company."

"Oh." She hesitated. "All right. Why don't you come inside?" She fumbled with the screen door for a while and Trace realized that it had two locks on it.

The house was as mousy and bland as its mistress. The living room looked as if it had been transported, whole, from the display window of a furniture store that still sold a sofa and two chairs for less than three hundred dollars, and would, if you bargained hard, throw in a couple of wood-grained Formica end tables. The rug was a vague tan tweed color and the furniture, upholstered in an equally vague blue, was placed in a precise straight line against one wall. There was a fireplace, bordered with imitation brick and filled with electrical equipment designed to enable fiberglass logs to produce a light that looked red when viewed through cellophane. The few framed prints on the walls looked as if they came from a Sunday-newspaper magazine. Trace expected to find a print of President Franklin Delano Roosevelt.

The only attractive and personal touch in the room was a three-foot-by-two-foot tapestry of a unicorn hanging unframed on the far wall.

"I'm sorry. You said your name was . . . ?"

"Tracy. Devlin Tracy."

"Would you like coffee, Mr. Tracy? It's ready."

"Thank you," Trace said. Perhaps the smell of coffee wafting into his nostrils would eradicate the faint smell of pine cleanser that permeated the room.

Trace sank back into the uncomfortable couch. He lit a cigarette and flicked it on into the large plastic kidney-shaped ashtray on the plastic end table next to him.

Mrs. Collins was back a minute later with coffee in two plain white mugs on two plain white saucers. She carried the mugs and a plastic creamer and sugar bowl on a genuine-imitation plastic rendition of an old-fashioned beer tray. Two stainless-steel spoons that looked like giveaways at some theater's Bingo Night completed the set.

"Mabley told me what's going on," Trace said. "Have you heard from your husband yet?"

She seemed at first hesitant to answer. She sipped at her coffee, which she had laced with three spoons of sugar and a generous helping of milk. When she put the cup down, she looked at Trace with eyes that he thought really could have been lovely.

"No," she said. Her voice was very soft and seemed almost to tremble.

"How long has it been now?" Trace asked.

"Five days. Since Wednesday."

Trace sipped at the coffee, but it was too weak and he put it back down.

"Aren't you worried?" he asked.

"I'm very worried," she said. She hesitated for a moment, as if wondering if it would be appropriate to be outraged by Trace's question, but her mousy little character decided that outrage was too strong to show. "Of course I'm worried," she said.

"But you haven't gone to the police yet," Trace said mildly.

"I—oh, well—Mr. Tracy, my husband is a very stern man. If I told the police that he was missing and people found out, he'd be a laughingstock when he came home. I couldn't do that." She shook her head, agreeing with herself. "No. I couldn't do that."

"Suppose something's happened, though?" Trace said.

"And suppose nothing's happened? Thomas would just kill me if I embarrassed him."

"Has your husband gone off before like this?"

"Sometimes he goes away on business. Conventions and like that," she said.

"Without telling you, I mean," Trace said.

She paused for a moment. "Never for this long," she said. "I always know where he's going and how long he'll be away."

"So this time's different. Don't you think that justifies a phone call to the police?"

"I don't know, Mr. Tracy. I don't know. How would you feel if your wife called the police on you?"

"She used to call the police on me all the time," Trace said. "That was one of the reasons I left."

"Well, I wouldn't involve Thomas," she said firmly. "He doesn't like disorder in his life, and he certainly wouldn't tolerate being embarrassed."

"What *does* Thomas like in his life?" Trace asked.

"What do you mean?"

"You know. The real him. I don't know anything about your husband. What is Thomas Collins like? I know he's a real-estate man, but what are his hobbies? Is he off hang-gliding somewhere in Alaska? What does he do when he's not in the office?"

"Real estate is actually his whole life, Mr. Tracy."

"Call me Trace. No hobbies? At night he sits around here and makes real-estate deals?"

"You're joking, but that's almost right. He reads site plans and maps and sits with his calculator and figures out cost estimates or whatever it is real-estate people do."

"Must be dull for you," Trace said.

"Not really. I have my art. I do tapestries, Mr. Tracy, and now there is finally some demand for my work."

"Is that one of yours?" Trace pointed to the hanging on the far wall. The woman nodded and Trace said, "I don't know anything about it, but I can tell it's very good work."

"It better be," she said. "It has to send our daughter through college." She seemed embarrassed at the praise, because a faint blush colored her cheeks.

"Was Thomas working on any special proj-

ect that might have taken him out of town?"
Trace asked.

"I don't know. We never discussed his business."

"He has a partner, doesn't he?"

"Yes. Rafe Rose. Collins and Rose."

"Did you talk to him?"

"About what?"

"About your husband being missing?" Trace
said.

"Yes. I called him Friday. He said he hadn't
seen Thomas since Wednesday afternoon. I
saw him Wednesday morning. He said he was
probably out putting together some kind of
deal."

"Doesn't his being absent like that gum up
his office's schedule? I mean, can the boss
afford to take that much time off?" Trace asked.

She shook her head. "Rafe and Thomas work
differently from most partners, I guess. Rafe
handles the office and the day-to-day business
of real estate."

"And your husband?"

"From what I gather, he's more involved in
putting together deals. He'll find somebody
who wants to build a shopping center and
someone else who owns property that would
be good for a mall, and he'll get a builder
who'll take a percentage of ownership in place
of a part of his fee, and he works out a package that meets everyone's needs. He spends
many days here on the telephone rather than
in the office. He says he can work just as well

here as there. Better, because the phones aren't always ringing."

"Does your husband have an office in the house?" Trace asked.

"Yes."

"Did you look at it? Does he keep an appointment book that might show he was going out of town?" Trace asked.

"I looked very carefully, Mr. Tracy, but I couldn't find anything. Would you like to see the office?"

"No. I couldn'd find anything that you didn't find. When did you see Thomas last?"

"Wednesday morning. He made himself coffee and drove off."

"He didn't say where he was going?"

"No."

"Is that your car in the driveway?" Trace asked, thinking of the ancient rusty Duster.

"Yes. Thomas has a black Corvette," she said.

"And he went to the office, 'cause they saw him in the afternoon, but no one knows where he's gone since then?" Trace said.

"That's correct."

"You said you had a daughter. Any other children?"

"No, just Tammy." She rose and walked to the cheap bookshelves that were against one wall and brought back a framed picture.

"You don't look old enough to have a college-age daughter," Trace said.

"Tammy's twenty. She was born when I

was very young, my first marriage. My husband died. Thomas and I have been married eight years." She handed the photograph to Trace, who saw that Tammy looked like she would turn into the woman her mother might have been. Even in the home snapshot, her hair was a flame red, swirling lightly about her face. There was something sensuous and mocking in the eyes, and she looked to Trace like a younger version of Ann-Margaret.

He handed the picture back. "She's very beautiful. Has she heard from Thomas?"

"No. She went back to school two weeks ago. Hollyhope College. I talk to her on the telephone most nights."

"And she hasn't heard from her stepfather?"

"I didn't even mention to her that he wasn't here. I didn't want to burden her with it."

"I think you should burden someone with it."

"I couldn't tell anybody. Not yet," she said.

"I think you should call the police."

"Definitely not."

"How worried are you about your husband?" Trace asked.

"I don't want to humiliate him."

"When your worry about him is bigger than your fear of embarrassing him, then you should call the police," Trace said.

"Mr. Mabley said that you were a detective."

"I'm an investigator," Trace said. "That's different."

"Oh?"

"Yes. Detectives carry guns and get in fist-fights and have a philosophy of life, a moral code."

"And you don't have a philosophy of life?"

"Oh, I do. It goes, Don't get involved," Trace said.

"I thought you might get involved in looking for Thomas. Just discreetly, you understand. Ask a few questions. Then if he comes back tomorrow or the next day, the newspapers, you know, no one would be saying Thomas Collins vanished and returns. When he comes back, you could just stop working."

"And if he doesn't come back?"

"Then you might be able to find him. Or if you thought it was really necessary, then I'd go to the police."

"I don't think so," Trace said. "There's the matter of my expenses."

"I don't have much money, but I'd be glad to pay you for your time," she said.

Trace shook his head. "You see, I'm in San Francisco on a convention, a vacation. I'm not really working."

"An insurance convention?"

"No. A Japanese-American convention," Trace said.

"That must be very interesting."

"I can tell you've never been to one," Trace said. "No, I'm sorry. Think about calling the police."

"Thank you for your concern, Mr. Tracy."

Their coffeecups were empty and Trace rose

to leave. At the front door, he saw a small black-and-white framed snapshot on a table inside the door.

It was of a man with thinning gray hair blowing around his head like some leftwing lawyer's. His nose was thin and needlelike, and his eyes were squinting menacingly.

"This Thomas?" Trace asked the woman.

"Yes?"

"I hope you get him back," Trace said.

Just before he got into his car, he clicked off the tape recorder on his hip.

6

When Trace got back to the hotel, the door connecting his room with Chico's was open but her room was empty. He found a note in an envelope pasted to his dresser mirror.

It read: "Wanna tlick? Wait around at 3 o'crock. Honorable mother will be otherwise engaged."

It was already two-thirty, so Trace showered quickly. When he came out, he carefully put his tape recorder away in the back of a drawer on top of the copy of Thomas Collins' insurance policy that Mabley had given him. He would have no more use for the frog microphone on this trip.

Case closed. A sappy woman with a sappy husband. He was so dumb he wandered away without telling anybody; she was so dumb she wouldn't call the police for fear of embarrassing him. And Trace was brought into the thing by Michael Mabley, who was so dumb that he was a friend of Walter Marks.

No thank you, no thank you, no thank you. He was off the case.

Trace wrapped a towel around himself and found the ice-cube machine down the hall. Then he poured himself a glass of Finlandia. It gave Trace a deep sense of satisfaction to note that even after several generous servings the bottle was still almost full. To a weary worker little things, like a stocked bar, meant a lot. He sat at the small table in the room and flicked on the television.

When Chico came in at ten after three, Trace was watching *The Dating Game*.

"Pick bachelor number one," he shouted.

"Why?" Chico said.

Trace turned, surprised to see her. He hadn't heard her come into the room.

"You've been here only a day and already you're becoming stealthy," he said. "Is it three o'clock already?"

"Ten after. Why should she pick bachelor number one? He looks like an ax murderer."

"Exactly. This show is bound to end in a disaster someplace. I just want to be sure I'm tuned in when the inevitable happens. 'We'll fly the two of you first class to Montezuma's Revenge Hotel in sunny Acapulco. But only one of you will return.'" Trace did his best *Revenge of the Fangman* laugh. "Actually, I've always wanted to be a contestant."

"Nobody'd ever pick you," Chico said.

"Who cares? I just want to answer the questions. 'What are your hobbies, Bachelor Number One?' Necrophilia and needlepoint and raising pit dogs. 'Very nice, Bachelor Number One. Will you bay at the moon for me?' Only if you're as big a dog as I think you are."

Chico flicked off the television set. "It must have been some day if you're sitting here taking out your frustration on game-show contestants."

"It was an awful day. Where's the mother?"

"She's gone to this terribly dismal lecture on productivity in automobile plants in a changing world," Chico said.

"Why? Your mother's a painter, for God's sakes."

"It's inherent in our souls," Chico said. "All Japanese want to become more efficient. I'm sure Mother thinks if she can find out how to put a fender on a car in twenty-seven seconds flat, somehow it's going to make her turn out a painting in four days instead of seven."

"Why don't you take your clothes off while we discuss this mania? I think it reflects a deep sexual need on your part," Trace said.

"Your place or mine?" Chico said.

"Well, as long as we're here."

They got into the bed, but then Chico bounded over and opened the window. Fresh air swirled through the room.

"I'll get pneumonia," Trace said.

"Breathe deep. It's good for you."

"Shouldn't we close that door between the rooms?"

"Mother won't be back."

"Suppose the lecture's dull?" Trace said. "Even for her."

"She still wouldn't leave," Chico said. "It is considered very insulting to walk out before the lecture is done."

"Very logical, but close the door anyway. I have this vision of not just your mother coming back but everybody in the convention with her. She'll be leading them like a Japanese tour through a casino. She'll have a yellow balloon on a stick and she'll be holding it over her head so everyone can follow it without getting lost and they'll all come marching through the room taking pictures and smiling at us. Why do Japanese always smile?"

"Because they know you roundeyes are inherently funny," Chico said. She locked the door and returned to bed.

Trace said, "By the way, what's black and goes *crick-crick* in the forest?"

"I don't know. I give up."

"You have no fighting heart," he said. "A Japanese camera left over from *Mr. Moto Takes a Photo*."

"You need a new writer," Chico said. "Why was your day awful?"

"I was doing Walter Marks a favor," Trace said.

"Hell, *that'd* ruin Mother Theresa's day."

"So I went to talk to a wife whose husband is missing but she won't call the cops 'cause she's afraid that when he turns up he'll turn up mad."

"What'd you do?"

"I told her to call the cops," Trace said.

"What'd she say?"

"She wanted me to investigate."

"What'd you say?" Chico asked, rubbing his bare stomach.

"Make bigger circles," Trace said. "I said no. I said that I was busy at this very interesting convention with the two women I love best in the world."

"Your mother and ex-wife will be interested in hearing that," Chico said.

"If you keep your little Oriental mouth closed, they'll never know."

"You really want me to keep my mouth closed?"

"Well, now that you mention it . . ." Trace rolled over toward her, but Chico was bounding out of bed. She started dressing.

"What . . ." Trace started, but she raised a finger for silence.

"Listen. The mother is back," she said. "I've got to go."

Trace rolled over and turned his back to her. "What is this?" Trace asked. "A lesson in 'Effective Contraception in a Changing World?'"

Seating at the convention's opening night dinner had been arranged by chance; people just happened to sit at tables where there was enough room for their party. That was the end of chance, Trace realized. From now on the Japanese regarded the seating arrangements as sacred, so Trace again found himself next to the man from Bataan, Mr. Nishimoto.

He smiled a lot at Trace except when he was paying attention to the speeches, which were all in Japanese and all interminable. Everybody in the audience sat in rapt attention and nodded politely at what Trace guessed was the end of each sentence.

Trace looked to Chico for salvation. "What are they talking about?"

"Corporate responsibility in an irresponsible changing world."

"Why do all the speeches sound alike?" Trace said.

"They *are* all alike," Chico said. "Japan has only one speechwriter for hire. He writes speeches like insurance policies, the same language over and over again."

Then Trace felt an all-too-familiar heavy hand on his arm. Mr. Nishimoto leaned toward him, smiling sincerely. He said, "Bataan. Sorry I missed you." Trace excused himself to the refuge of the men's room. When he came back, he found the elderly Japanese in Trace's chair talking to Chico. He vacated for Trace with an obliging grin.

"What's he always talking to you about anyway?" Trace asked Chico.

"He tells me how much he likes you," Chico said. "And my mother."

"Oh." Trace drained his sake cup. "I like him, too."

"And what about me?" Chico countered. "Or is that a roll of quarters in your pocket?"

"Mercury dimes. Sorry. But we can divvy up in my room."

When the telephone rang, Trace rolled over. Before the sheets could settle, it britzed again, sounding off in that particularly vicious way that hotel telephones have of ringing. Trace put his pillow on his head. Once more into the britz and he growled to Chico, "For crying out loud, answer the phone."

When it rang again, he prodded the tangle of blankets next to him but it didn't respond. Then he remembered that Chico had come upstairs with him last night, but then gone next door to sleep in her mother's room.

"This better be good," he mumbled, throwing one arm toward the sound. Despite the shuffling and clunking of the flotsam that cluttered the bedside table, Trace resolutely refused to open his eyes. He knew that eyes, once opened, would not close again in peaceful rest until a day had passed. And the self-imposed handicap often provided enough of a delay to cause any caller to hang up in frustration. But not this time.

"Trace," an unfamiliar voice said.

"What is this, bed check? Who are you?"

"This is Mike Mabley."

"I bet you've been up for hours," Trace said.

"I heard from Judith Collins."

Trace screwed his eyes shut tighter and said nothing.

Mabley continued, "I think you should talk to her today."

"Why?" Trace mumbled. It was all too clear to him now; he wasn't going to be allowed to go back to sleep. He cracked one eye open.

"She thinks she knows something about her husband," Mabley said.

"If she doesn't, who does?"

"About his disappearance."

"If she's got anything, she ought to go to the cops. I told her that."

"She won't do that," Mabley said. "Please, Trace. Talk to her. Maybe you can talk her into it. She was very impressed with you yesterday."

No use. Trace was awake now, for good. He got up and flicked on the television. "Wait a minute," he coughed into the phone and straggled into the bathroom to use mouthwash. He thought Paul Newman should invent industrial-strength mouthwash for mornings after like this.

Bolstered by the chemical rinse, Trace was now ready to refuse Mabley. He glanced at the television. The in-house channel was presenting, in glorious green-tinged color, the fabulous events going on in the hotel that day.

The featured event seemed to be the Japanese-American convention, its essence condensed on videotape to a panoramic view of conventioneers happily chewing their octopus. The camera then fired on Trace's dinner partner, Mr. Nishimoto, who stared directly into its lens smiling. Bataan's champion then began looking around as if something were missing.

He's looking for me, Trace thought. I'm not even out of bed yet and he's looking for me.

Still glued to the screen, he picked up the phone again and said, "Tell her I'll be there when I can get there."

"Thanks, Trace," Mabley said.

"Don't mention it."

7

"The day at the farm was super. In case you were looking for it, I found this in my bag when you brought me back. When do we play hot tub again? Mandy."

The note was written on a sheet of pulpy white note paper. The envelope was the common kind bought in drugstores and there was no return address. The note had been printed in black ballpoint ink.

Trace handed the note back. "What came with this?" he asked Judith Collins.

She handed him a square silver cuff link with the initials T.C. on it.

"Your husband's?" Trace said.

"Yes."

"And it was in the envelope?"

She nodded.

"When did you get this letter?"

"I got it at the post office. I was looking in Thomas' desk for, well, maybe an appointment listing or an airline reservation or something, and I found a key for the postal box in town. I went down there and found this letter in the box."

"Did you know he had this box?" Trace asked.

"No. This was the first I knew of it," she said. Trace looked at the post-box key. It was one of the big heavy ones that the postal service used. The top of it, above the small keychain hole, was scratched.

"Who's Mandy?" Trace asked as he put the key down on the coffee table between them.

"I don't know. I never heard her name before."

"The envelope is postmarked San Francisco too," Trace said. "You never heard him mention any Mandy in San Francisco? Maybe somebody he worked with or was doing business with?"

"You mean hot-tub business?" she said sharply. The woman paused to regain control of herself. "I never heard of her."

"Still no word from your husband?"

"No. Nothing."

"Did you find the other cuff link?" Trace asked.

Her green eyes opened wide as she looked at Trace, surprised at something she hadn't thought of. "I'll look now."

When she left the living room, Trace looked at the note again. Unfortunately, there didn't seem to be anything significant about it. He always wished that he could solve a mystery someday by seeing something that the poor dumb plodding police had overlooked. "I'm sorry, Inspector, but Lady Watercloset couldn't have written that letter. You see, it accuses her husband of not being honorable. But honor is spelled without a 'u.' Lady Watercloset wouldn't have done that. Inspector, this letter is a fake, written by an American to throw you off the track." "My God, Mister Trace, I never thought of that. And the only American who could have written it was . . ." "Exactly. Dina Davenport. I think if you check, Inspector, you'll see that . . ."

Judith Collins reappeared beside the tacky sofa. "It isn't there," she said. "Thomas keeps his cuff links in a special box on the dresser, but it's not there." She saw Trace nod and said, "Is it important?"

"I don't know. I just thought that if it was there, then he might have lost this cuff link weeks ago. But if it wasn't, maybe he lost it since he left home last Wednesday. I don't know."

"I see."

"Mrs. Collins, does your husband cheat on you?"

The woman settled into a chair, looked down at her chest, and started to cry softly.

"I'm sorry," Trace said.

She wiped her eyes. "And I'm sorry," she said. "I don't know. The letter certainly makes it look like he cheated on me, doesn't it?"

"You never had reason to suspect him before?" Trace said. "I remember you telling me he's out of town on business a lot."

"But I could reach him. I knew where he was and I never would have thought twice about calling his room, wherever he was staying." She put her handkerchief away and lifted her teacup. "A wife usually knows, Mr. Tracy, when her husband cheats. I don't think Thomas was cheating on me. Until this note. Now I don't know."

"He might be?" Trace said.

"Isn't it obvious?" she answered.

"Where's the farm?" Trace asked.

For a moment, she looked confused and Trace lifted the note signed Mandy "This farm," he said.

"I don't know."

"You don't own a farm?" Trace asked.

"No."

"A friend, then? Maybe your husband and this Mandy were together at somebody else's farm. Do you have any friends who have a farm?"

"No. I can't think of any," she said.

"I think you ought to go to the police now," Trace said.

"I just can't. Certainly not after getting this note. Thomas would go crazy."

"Why'd you have Mabley call me?"

The woman shrugged with her whole body. "I don't know. But you are the only two people in the world who know that Thomas is gone."

"The neighbors haven't asked questions?" Trace asked.

"I'm not close to any of them. And they're used to Thomas being out of town. Mr. Tracy, I'd like to hire you for one day. See if you can find out anything. I promise you, if you don't find out where Thomas is, then I'll call the police."

"He's been gone a week. You should have called them a long time ago."

"Just give me one day," she said.

Trace shook his head. "You don't understand," he said. "You seem to think that I'm some kind of real detective who can found out things like that." He snapped his fingers.

"Then what are you?" she asked.

"I'm a bumbler. I fumble around. I never figure anything out. I just annoy people. I never catch anybody. I'm not a detective, I'm an annoyance clerk. I should work in a department store."

Mrs. Collins stared at Trace for a long time. Then her shoulders shuddered as if from an explosion deep within her body, and she dropped her head toward her chest and began to sob uncontrollably. "Please, Mr. Tracy. Please."

Trace sighed. He could never resist good manners.

8

The Collins-Rose Real Estate Developers, Inc.
office was sunken into a small shopping mall
that was hidden in a corner of San Francisco
near the Golden Gate Bridge. Apparently the
mall was one of those places where kids con-
gregated at night because the parking lot was
littered with empty beer cans. In San Francisco, as elsewhere, police seemed to have
adopted a hands-off policy where normally
active adolescents were concerned. In an empty
parking lot teenage morons don't bother anybody but themselves.

Collins' office was surrounded by entrepre-
neurial originality. On one side was a place
that advertised the best alfalfa cookies in the
world, and on the other, a video store that
offered a full weekend of sex for six dollars,
with club membership.

Trace looked in the video-store window and
a woman at a checkout counter inside yelled

out at him. "Why you looking in the window? Come on in. Only six dollars."

Trace looked at the woman. She had all the charm of a laundry hamper. He said, "I usually get more than six dollars."

"Smartass," she said. "Faggot."

But once inside the Collins-Rose office, he met a girl for whom he would gladly waive his usual six-dollar weekend fee. She was a tall blond with sun-warmed skin and blue eyes as light as thick ice. She was enough to make a man want to take up surfing.

The nameplate on her desk read LAURIE ANDERS and Trace marveled at another California name. Where were all the ethnics in California? What happened to all the Carluccis?

"May I help you?"

"I'd like to see Mr. Rose," Trace said.

"Do you have an appointment?"

"No."

"He is in a meeting right now. What does it concern? Perhaps one of our salesmen could help you?"

"I don't think so," Trace said. "It's a personal matter. I'm a friend of Mrs. Collins."

"Oh," she said, and Trace thought a faint cloud drifted over the sunlight of her face.

"If you want to wait, I think Mr. Rose should be free soon," she said.

Trace followed her gaze to a sofa alongside the wall near the door. He sat down, flipped through the stack of magazines. He had read them all. He glanced up to catch the young woman looking at him.

"Is Mr. Collins in today?" he asked casually.

She shook her head. "I didn't ask your name," she said.

Trace gave her one of his business cards and asked if he could get her some coffee.

"No," she said.

"Then can I go next door and get you a movie?"

"No, thanks," she said and rose from the desk and walked toward the back of the building with his business card in her hand.

Trace was back on the couch when she returned a few minutes later. "Mr. Rose can see you now," she said.

"Thank you." He followed the young woman, who wiggled her way down a long corridor, past a lot of small cubbyhole offices like the kind salesmen had at a new-car agency.

"I'm glad you didn't say 'walk this way,'" Trace said.

"I know, you'd throw a hip out of joint," she said. "I know that Groucho Marx joke."

"How about Chico?" Trace said. "I can play the piano just like Chico Marx. You got two lemons, I'll show you."

"We don't have a piano," she said.

"It's just as good on a desk. I play the desk with lemons and I'm real good at it, even if it did put an end to my business career."

"How about Harpo?" she said.

"How's that?" he asked.

"No talk," she said.

"Well, if you're going to be that way about it," Trace said.

She led him into an office where a dark-haired man wearing an immaculate pin-striped suit with a lightly figured dark tie sat at one side of a long conference table facing the door.

"This is Mr. Tracy," Laurie said. Trace noticed that he was holding Trace's business card.

"Thank you. Mr. Tracy, would you like some coffee?" Rose asked.

"No, I can't play the desk with coffee. Only lemons," Trace said.

"Excuse me?"

"Never mind," Trace said. He noticed Laurie was smiling.

"Thank you, Laurie, that'll be all," Rose said. He did not stand up, nor did he offer his hand to Trace. His fingernails were manicured and shiny, and Trace had the suspicion that Rafe Rose might be a health and cleanliness freak who did not shake hands with anybody for fear of contracting an incurable disease.

"Laurie said you're a friend of Mrs. Collins?" Rose said.

"An acquaintance," Trace corrected.

"You live around here?"

"No. Las Vegas."

"Well, any acquaintance of et cetera, et cetera," Rose said. Not a hint of a smile flickered across his face, though, Trace noticed. "So what can I do for you?"

"Mrs. Collins asked me to look for her husband," Trace said.

"He's not home? That's where he usually is," Rose said.

"I think she'd know if he was home," Trace said. "Doesn't he spend much time in the office?"

"No, he goes long stretches without being in here at all. Just what's this all about. Where's Judith?"

"Judith is home. She hasn't seen her husband in a week," Trace said. "I told her I'd look for him."

Rose's face wrinkled up around the eyes. "This might be serious," he said, "couldn't it?"

Trace nodded.

"Did she call the police? They haven't been here," Rose said.

"I think she's afraid to. She acts a little bit timid where her husband's concerned."

"I can understand that," Rose said. "Hold on." He dialed two digits on the phone and said, "Laurie, when was the last time you talked to Thomas?" He nodded and said, "Do you know of any appointments he's had out of town this past week? I want to reach him."

He waited a while, said thanks, and hung up.

"Laurie's our office manager but she doubles as Thomas's secretary when he's in the office. But she hasn't talked to him in a week and she doesn't know of any appointments

he's lined up. You know, Judith called me last
week and asked if Thomas was here. I didn't
think it was important."

"Maybe it isn't yet," Trace said. "Was Collins working on anything special that you know
about? Something that might have taken him
out of town?"

"Thomas is pretty closemouthed. He usually comes in with a deal only after he's put it
all together, and *then* we fight about it. So I
wouldn't normally know about anything special he was doing."

"It sounds to me like you do most of the
work around here," Trace said.

Rose shrugged. "I put in the most hours,
that's for sure. But Thomas's deals make lot of
money, probably the biggest part of our income.
So it works out."

"How long have you two been partners?"
Trace asked.

"Eleven years. We both had small agencies
and we merged them. I took over the straight
day-to-day stuff and Thomas got the big jobs."

"You think it's fair?"

Rose nodded. "We're both doing a lot better
than we were doing on our own. I'm sorry,
Mr. Tracy, I wish I could tell you where the
hell Thomas is."

"Maybe you'd like to call Mrs. Collins and
have her verify that I'm here on her behalf,"
Trace said.

"Why? I don't have any reason to doubt
you."

"Okay. I just wanted you to have the opportunity," Trace said, "because sometimes questions get sticky?"

"Such as?" Rose asked.

"Does Collins fool around? Does he have a girlfriend maybe stashed somewhere, where he might be hiding out sick or something?"

Rose spun around and looked at the wall where certificates in a half-dozen real-estate organizations were framed and hung. Then he spun slowly back to Trace.

"All right," he said. "Thomas would screw a snake if he could get his body low enough. He does a lot of business trips, but he does a lot more trips just to play around. Fact is, I always envied him. He goes off to Las Vegas, makes believe it's a business trip, and winds up in the sack with somebody for the weekend. I'd do it if I didn't think my wife would find out and kill me. He's a world-class swordsman, Mr. Tracy. Does that help?"

"It'd help more if you could point me toward a couple of his scabbards," Trace said.

"You never know with Thomas," Rose said. "None of them matters to him. I mean, women are just women. He doesn't talk about them a lot except, well, you know, to brag about somebody's tits or something. Usual locker-room talk. I couldn't give you a name."

"Are his women always out of town?" Trace asked. "Maybe he's got somebody stashed here in the city?"

"He could have, but I wouldn't know," Rose said.

"How about in the office? He have anybody around here? What about Laurie? Does she have a little romance going?"

For a moment Rose's face looked puzzled, as if he were considering the possibility for the first time and not liking it. Finally he said, "I don't think so. And not Laurie. She just doesn't like Thomas at all."

"She ever say that?"

"She doesn't have to. He's always passing remarks about her ass or legs or something, and I can tell she doesn't care for it. And there's nobody else in the office that Thomas'd fool around with. He told me once, you know, you start bopping your secretary and ten days later your wife knows about it because your secretary suddenly starts sounding different on the phone. Women can't help hinting, he said."

"Probably true," Trace said. "Men brag and women hint; it all works out the same. Anybody screws anybody and everybody knows about it. You ever hear him talk about a girl named Mandy?"

"Can't say that I have," Rose said.

"You know anything about any farm he might visit or might go to? Or any friend of his who owns a farm?"

Rose looked puzzled again. He had a way of wrinkling up the corners of his eyes when he did not feel comfortable with questions, but he answered quickly. "No. But I do know that those are pretty specific questions coming from somebody who claims he doesn't know anything about Thomas' whereabouts."

"There was a note from somebody named Mandy. It talked about meeting Collins on a farm somewhere. A farm with a hot tub."

"I don't know anything about it," Rose said.

"Do you think Laurie might?"

"Maybe. She doesn't do much else for Thomas except take his phone calls, but you could ask her. Should I call her in?"

Trace glanced at his watch. "No," he said. "Just don't complain if she goes to lunch with me."

"You want me to be your dating service?" Rose asked with a smile.

"I don't think that'll be necessary with my charm," Trace said.

"Okay. Are you going to tell her that Thomas has taken a powder?"

"Not if I can help it," Trace said. He rose and walked to the door. "One last thing," he told the real-estate man.

"Sure. What's that?"

"Why is everyone so formal about Collins? Why do they all call him Thomas?"

"Would you want to be called Tom Collins?" Rose asked.

"It's not so bad. I knew a stripper once named Brandy Alexander," Trace said.

9

The only way Laurie Anders could get Trace to enter the lemon-bright restaurant that bragged of "fresh bean sprouts daily" was to assure him that the bar served real alcoholic drinks.

The place was a little touch of Old New York, Trace thought. Because the walls were of Formica and the ceiling of wood and there wasn't a drape or a rug or anything in the place that could absorb or muffle noise, it sounded like the kitchen on a Chinese passenger boat—or the old Sardi's. The only difference was that in New York they packed the tables close together, and here in California at least there was enough distance between the small tables so that your elbow didn't wind up in somebody else's blue-cheese dressing.

Trace hated the place. It was too bright, too noisy, and too damned self-consciously cheery for a man who spent his lunchtime just a little bit depressed in a room with a dungeon atmosphere. A little dampness wouldn't hurt either, he decided. Every restaurant should have a small leak in the cellar. Sneaky as ever, he turned on his tape recorder.

"Is Laurie Anders your real name?"

"Of course. Why?"

"It's like a California name. Something from a marquee. I was hoping you'd tell me your name was really Angelina Baccigalupa."

"Sorry," she said. "The name's real. Everything in California is real, didn't you know that?"

"Somehow that must have slid by me," Trace said. "Did Mr. Rose order you to talk to me?"

"No. After I chased you out of the office, he ordered me to go to lunch with you. He didn't say anything about talking. I was very upset, you know."

"God, I'm not that homely," Trace said.

"No, it sounded like 'entertain the big spender from out of town.' I don't do that kind of work."

"Set your mind at ease," Trace said. "I'm not a big spender from anywhere. Actually, I've been figuring out how to stick you with the lunch tab. Did Rose tell you what I want?"

"No. He just asked me to try to be helpful. That's what got my back up," Laurie said.

"You figured I was going to whisk you off to the Econoline Six Motel for two hours of fun and frolic?"

"Something like that," she said.

"I don't go anyplace that I can't rent for at least three hours," Trace said.

"Your women must be very happy," she said.

Trace shook his head. "Actually it's that it takes me two and a half hours to sober up."

The young woman really did have marvelously blue eyes, and sitting across from her, Trace could catch the faint scent of her perfume. It was a natural fresh smell. Too much perfume smelled like rancid flower paste. Trace liked perfumes that reminded him of trees and meadows, soft breezes and warm sunlight, especially since perfume was usually as close as he got to trees, meadows, breezes, or sunlight.

"What *are* you taking me to lunch for? *And* picking up the check," Laurie asked. Her voice was as gentle as her good looks. She wore a beige blouse and a brown skirt that hugged her hips tightly. That was another thing he hated: balloon skirts that made women's shapes look like tufted pin-cushions.

"I've come to put you into movies," Trace said.

"Somebody's told you about my kazoo solos? News really travels fast out here. Come on, sell me an insurance policy and let me go back to work."

"I'm an investigator," Trace said. "Well, sort of an investigator."

"I saw your business card. You're with Garrison Fidelity," Laurie said.

"I investigate things for them once in a while when I'm feeling up to it."

"And you're feeling up to it now, is that it?"

"Yeah. I'm looking for Thomas Collins," Trace said. "And I know, I should look for him home but he's not home and nobody's seen him for a week. I thought you might be of some help to me."

"I haven't seen him for a week either," she said. "Does making it unanimous help you at all?"

"Not much," Trace said. Laurie had a faint smile on her face; it was the look worn by women who were beautiful, had always been beautiful, and had always been accustomed to wrapping men around their fingers. Trace did not care for it.

"Did he tell you he was going out of town or anything like that?" he asked.

"No," she said, dawdling with her fork over the large chef's salad she had ordered, an unappetizing mixture of apparently inedible objects that looked like wine-bottle corks and frogs' entrails. She looked up again, fixing him with her clear cold eyes.

"Is he really a missing-type person? Are the police going to find him in fifteen years suffering from amnesia and living in Dubuque?"

"Police haven't been called. They may never find him anywhere," Trace said.

"Isn't that odd? Not calling the police?" she asked.

"I think she's afraid of ticking him off if he's just away on business. Speaking of which, you double as his secretary, right?"

"I take his messages. When he's in the office, which isn't very often, I do some typing for him."

"Would you know if he was going out of town?" Trace asked.

"Nobody knows anything about where he goes and what he does. He doesn't even tell Mr. Rose, so he wouldn't tell me."

"You know nothing? You mean I'm spending three dollars on this rabbit food and it's going to be a total waste," Trace said.

"I'm afraid it looks that way," she said.

"Do you think he might have gone to the farm?" Trace asked.

"Not for a whole week," she said.

"Why not?"

"I get the idea it's a place he uses only . . . well, once in a while, you know, just overnight."

"Have you been there?" Trace asked.

The young woman blushed for a moment, not quite as confident-looking as she had been a few minutes before, and said, "I refuse to answer on the grounds that my answers might tend to involve me."

"Is the farm his?" Trace asked.

"I guess so. I never asked."

"You know, his wife and partner don't know anything about it," Trace said.

"About what?"

"About Collins owning a farm."

"How'd you know, then?" Laurie asked.

"You just told me," Trace said.

The young woman took a sip of her Perrier. "And here I thought you were just another pretty face," she said.

"Behind this pretty face lurks a mind like a steel trap," Trace said. "Tell me about the farm."

"Must I? It's—it's tacky."

"Me or eventually the police," Trace said. "I'm a better bet. Where is the farm?"

"Over the bridge about a half-hour. Near a place called Nicasio. It's just a small place, a little house, a couple of outbuildings. It doesn't grow anything."

"Why'd he buy it?" Trace asked.

"You don't know?" Trace shook his head, and she said, "Maybe you're not so smart after all. Thomas uses it to fool around. He brings women there."

"And you were one of the women," Trace said, speaking softly, making sure there was no accusation in his voice, only a flat statement of fact.

"Just once," she said.

"When was that?"

"About a year ago, right after he got the place."

"Was that the only time you ever slept with him?" Trace asked.

"Yes."

"How did he keep his hands off you? Rose told me what kind of guy he is. How could he not be all over you?"

"He is all over me," she said. "Since I first

came to work here, he's been pawing me, goosing me, propositioning me. At first I thought he was just another nerd and then I saw he was serious. Are you going to tell him anything I say?" she asked suddenly.

"Not a chance," Trace said. "Not him and not anybody else."

"I guess I believe you," she said. "Should I?"

"I'm the only game in town," Trace said.

She thought about that for a long while, long enough for Trace to wave to the waitress for another drink.

"Okay. Collins is a real mutt. He never lets up, he never stops hitting on you, no matter how much you tell him to back off, no matter how many times you say no. He's not above telling you that he's the boss and it would help you to be nice to him."

"If you feel that way, how'd you wind up there with him?"

"I stood him off for three years and then one night I weakened. I just broke up with a boyfriend; it was kind of messy and I was feeling punk. Thomas was in the office late that night and so was I, and well, one thing led to another."

"Why do you think he didn't tell anybody about it?" Trace asked.

Laurie shrugged. "If he told his wife about the farm, what good would it be to him?"

"Why not tell Rose? They're partners, after all. Do they have secrets?"

"I don't know," she said.

"What kind of women does Collins fool around with?" Trace asked.

"Ugly ones."

"Present company excepted," he said with a smile.

"You have to realize we weren't close," she said.

"That's a given. Anything you can tell me would be appreciated and kept quiet."

"He messes around with any woman who'll mess around with him," she said.

"Pros? Hookers?" Trace asked.

"I don't know. I wouldn't think so. I mean, the man's got a few bucks, I don't think he'd mess around with hookers. But waitresses, clerks, anybody, you name it, that man never stops sniffing."

"All one-night stands?" Trace asked. "What about romance? Long love affairs? Anything like that?"

"I don't know. We're hardly pals."

"How'd you stand him off after you went to the farm with him?" Trace asked.

"He came on to me after that like the Iranian army, swooping and screaming, but I told him no, never again, it was a mistake and leave me alone."

"And he did," Trace said.

"He never did. He was always after me, but I didn't bend."

"Did he ever talk about any other women? Do you remember any names?"

"He talked all the time, but never any names. You know, it was that kind of joke talk that a lounge lizard gives you with the raised eyebrows and the winks and all that crap, but always with a built-in out. Men like that can always tell a wife they were just joking. It was locker-room talk, embarrassing, from some guy on the make. I wonder if men know how women hate that kind of bull."

"Men who talk like that are too dumb to care," Trace said, feeling very noble. "Did he ever mention a woman named Mandy?"

"No. No names. Maybe sometime in his bragging he said something like that, but I wouldn't remember. Is there a reason?"

"I found a note that said somebody named Mandy was at the farm with him," Trace said.

"I'm sorry. The name doesn't mean anything to me."

"What do you think of Mrs. Collins?" Trace asked.

"She's your client. What can I say?"

"The truth is usually good," Trace said.

"All right. Look up the word 'mousy' in any dictionary and you'll see her picture. You know, if she calls the office, it's 'whisper, whisper, terribly sorry, don't disturb him but can she speak to Thomas if he's not busy.' That kind of thing."

"So she's not a friend that you can chitchat to on the telephone?"

"No. I see her once a year at office parties. Maybe twice if we have a picnic."

"She and Collins get along?" Trace asked.

"I guess so. I don't think her daughter likes Collins, though."

"Why do you say that?"

"She came to the office once with her mother when Thomas was there. Just the looks she gave him gave me that idea."

"What do *you* think of Collins?" Trace asked.

"I detest him," she said.

"How's the partnership going? With Rose. Are they making any money?"

"Mr. Rose is a great boss. I think he and Collins get along all right, but I don't know anything about making money. Mr. Rose is always complaining, but that's normal in the real-estate business."

"All right. The real important question," Trace said.

"What's that?"

"What's a nice girl like you doing in a place like this?"

"It's a good job and it's been paying my way through law school at night," she said.

"God. Another lawyer. Don't we have enough lawyers?"

"Not enough good ones. There's never enough good anything," she said.

"That's what I always tell my girlfriend. You graduating soon?"

"Another semester and I'll be clerking."

"Another thing," Trace said. "You've been real open and honest with me and you didn't have to be. How come?"

"No skin off my nose," she said. "What are they going to do, fire me? I've already given notice that I'm leaving at the end of the month."

Trace nodded and lunch dribbled away to small talk, another drink, and thanking her for her help.

Her real help was in verifying the existence of the farm and telling him where it was.

Now he wanted to go sit in a quiet bar somewhere and think about whether or not he wanted to do anything with that information.

10

Trace found Chico in the hotel cocktail lounge, where she was seated at a table in the corner, eating large handfuls of oyster crackers, sipping tea, and talking Japanese at the speed of light with Mr. Nishimoto.

When he saw Trace, he stood and bowed slightly. "Ahhh," he said. "Bataan. Sorry I missed you."

"The feeling's mutual," Trace said. "And, I hope we'll be missing each other again soon." He slid into the banquette next to Chico and Mr. Nishimoto bowed and walked quickly away.

"What does that man want?"

"I told you—he's interested in my mother," Chico said.

"If he's so interested in her, why doesn't he talk to her?"

"That would be rude," Chico said. "He is counting on me to let my mother know that he is interested in her. That way, if she is not interested, she can just continue to ignore him and she will not offend him by rejecting him."

"And if she is interested?" Trace said.

"Then she can be nice to him, without running the risk of being rejected herself and having to commit suicide," Chico said.

"That is just too goddamn inscrutable for me, and I thought that three years of living with you had made me real scrutable," Trace said.

"Trust me. It's the way it's done," Chico said.

"I don't like the idea of you fixing your mother up," he said.

"Why not?"

"Suppose she gets the idea to do the same for you?" he said. "Then where am I?"

"Hold that thought, barbarian," she said.

Chico had finished all the fish crackers and Trace asked the waitress for more, along with a double vodka on the rocks.

"Where have you been?" she asked as he sipped from his drink.

"I was bored with this place, so I went out on the street to see if I could get lucky with one of these northern California beauties, but the two other straight guys in town had everything booked up for the day, so I came back here to you."

"Should I be flattered?"

"And I thought, Trace, I thought, why are you fooling around looking for hamburger when you've got sirloin back at the hotel. That's what I thought, I really did."

"I've never been called a piece of meat with such éclat," she said.

"You have a knack for seeing the dark side of everything," he said. "Anyway, I thought to myself, Why don't you go rescue your honey, who must be tired by now of this convention and who probably needs a break, and why don't you take her for a ride in the beautiful California countryside?"

"The grand gesture," she said. "I love it. Let's go."

"Will your mother be all right?" he asked.

"Yes. She's at a lecture on flower arranging in a changing world."

"Mmmm, sure you want to miss it?"

Trace loved driving in San Francisco. The first time he had ever been in the city, he had been walking somewhere from his hotel. Like most New Yorkers, he had stepped off the curb to get a head start crossing the street before the light changed. Instantly, cars coming from all four directions came to a screeching halt. Trace was perplexed: a tank blockade set up by transvestites couldn't stop traffic in Manhattan. But a man standing next to him explained, "They stopped because you stepped onto the street."

Trace hopped back onto the curb and the traffic roared to life again. This nearly mystical knowledge gave him a wonderfully insane sense of power and Trace took to Alphonse-and-Gastoning traffic as a hobby: "After you!" "No, please—after *you*. I insist." Gridlock for miles.

To take his pastime behind the wheel was a natural; every time he drove he kept looking around for people standing—even lying—in the gutter so he could stop and snarl traffic.

He was doing it now and Chico said, "When you said you were taking me for a drive, I didn't think you meant stopping at every corner."

"All right," he said. "A guy can't even have a little fun."

Driving over the Golden Gate Bridge, he told her about Thomas Collins, the note from Mandy, and his lunch with Laurie Anders.

"It sounds to me like he's left his wife," Chico said.

"I think so too," he said, "although I don't know where he's going to get a better deal. He's no prize, and his wife is a pushover. He's not going to find another one like her."

They drove out through Marin County and then turned off on a small road just before the town of Nicasio. Trace was trying to read road signs that were painted on concrete posts mounted at the corners, but the writing was sun-faded and dim and he couldn't make them out.

"I thought we were going for a drive," Chico said.

"What do you think we're doing, space-walking?"

"I think you're slowing down at each corner looking for something. That's not a drive, it's a mission."

"I'm looking for Collins' farm," he said. "I thought it might be nice to visit."

"Do you think he has goats and chickens?" she asked.

"Yes. And horses and donkeys and sheep and big moo-cows and a very mean bull that everybody must stay away from."

"Good. Where is the farm?"

"I don't know. I can't read the street signs," he said.

"Stop and ask for directions."

"That never works."

"What do you mean it never works?" Chico asked.

"Every time I stop and ask somebody for directions, he turns out to be the only person in three states who doesn't speak English. Or, if he does speak English, he just visiting here and doesn't know where any place is. Or if he speaks English and isn't just visiting here, he is sure to be the dumbest bastard who ever lived and he couldn't find his foot in his shoe without directions."

"Well, I'll ask," Chico said. "I'm real lucky. And here comes a live one."

Trace pulled off to the side of the road as a man on foot approached down the thin sliver of sidewalk.

"What's this place we're looking for?" Chico asked.

"It's called the old Walters farm. It's on Palmer Road."

"Just watch me," she said.

Chico rolled down the window, and as the man drew abreast of the car, she called out, "Excuse me, sir."

The man stopped and looked at her. He was in his sixties, and he was wearing a dark brown suit that was dirty and didn't fit. Under it was a tee-shirt.

"God is coming," the man intoned. "Will you be ready?"

Trace laughed. Chico jabbed him in the ribs with her pointy little elbow. "Shut up, heathen," she hissed.

"We're going to try to be ready. Really try," she told the man.

"It is too late. All are doomed." The man raised a hand over his head, pointing to the sky as if to show where doom came from.

"Well, if we're all doomed anyway," Chico said, "I can't think of a better place to be doomed than the old Walters farm on Palmer Road. Where is that place anyway?"

"There is no hiding," the man shouted.

"We're not going to hide there. We're just going to milk the cows before Armageddon," Chico said.

"Can I leave now?" Trace said.

"Not on your life. We're getting close. I can feel it," Chico said.

The man was still babbling, now about Armageddon.

"The old Walters farm. We're all meeting there. Where is it?" Chico asked the man.

He stopped in midsentence. "Who's all meeting there?"

"The children of the book," Chico said. "Oh, the power that is ours. The glory forever. Where is the old Walters farm?"

"The glory forever," the man said. He waved his arm down the road. "Down there on the right. A half-mile. It has a sign."

"Praise be," Chico said. "Thank you."

"The end is coming," the man said.

"And not a moment too soon," Chico said.

"Glory, glory," he said.

"Hallelujah, hallelujah," Chico said.

"Have a nice day," Trace shouted to the man, and drove off.

The farm was just where the lunatic said it would be, on the right, at the end of a long unpaved drive that led up a slight hillock to where the house stood overlooking the roadway.

There was no garage; the roadway just trickled to an end near the house. Off to the left side of the homestead, about thirty yards away, Trace saw a rickety frame building that looked, in size, like a cross between a barn and a utility shed. So far as he could tell, nothing was grown on the farm except fruit trees, and they looked as if they had been left to shift for themselves, with wildflowers and tall uncut grass growing high around their trunks.

"What are you looking for?" Chico asked.

"Collins' car. No sign of it. I guess he's not here," Trace said.

"All it shows is that his car's not here," Chico said. "Let's see if anybody's to home. That's what us country folk say. 'To home.'"

The front door faced the roadway. It was at ground level without even a single step for a porch. There was no answer to the doorbell and the door was locked.

They found another door around the back of the house. Looking through its glass panes, they could see it led into the kitchen, but also there was no answer and again the door was locked.

"Well, too bad," Trace said. "My only hope was that we'd luck out and find him up here."

"Yeah, too bad," Chico said. "Nice little house. Would you like to live in the country, Trace?"

"After all the bugs and mice move out," Trace said.

"Stupid. That's part of the charm of the country."

"If it's so charming, why did you threaten to kill the condo manager that time you discovered a mouse in the apartment?"

"That was different. That was a surly city mouse. Out here the mice are right out of Walt Disney. They sing you to sleep at night," Chico said.

"Well, that might be a welcome change," Trace said. "Someone pleasant to share my bedroom. It beats having two snoring Orientals in the next room."

"Aaaaah, you lack the romantic spirit, Trace."

"I have an excess of the romantic spirit. That's why I hate sleeping alone," he said.

Chico walked away from him back toward the front of the house. When he finally caught up with her, she was standing by the front door, wearing the evil smile he had come to know and distrust.

"Why are you smirking?"

"Come here, dummy," she said.

He stood alongside her by the door and she said, "If you were a housekey, where would you hide?"

Trace said, "Under the doormat."

"There is no doormat."

"In the milkbox, then," he said.

"Ditto the milk box."

"All right, no milk box. Then over the door. Definitely over the door."

"Reach up there and see for yourself," she said.

He ran his hand along the top of the door frame.

No key.

"That's the dumbest thing you've ever had me do," he said. "All I got were dirty fingers."

"Your whole thinking is rooted in the past,"

she said. "Today people don't keep keys under the mat or over the door."

"Where do they keep them?" he asked.

"They keep them in little artificial rocks. *Voilà.*"

She pulled her hand from behind her back. It held a gray stone just like the other gray stones that bordered some of the bushes that grew in front of the house. She turned the stone over in her mind. Underneath it was a thin circle of fiberglass, mounted at one end by a screw that was embedded in the stone.

She slid the fiberglass plate back to reveal a house key.

"Pretty smart," Trace said.

"Thank you." She handed him the key. "Go ahead. You break in. If neighbors call the cops, I don't want to be involved."

"You think you're so smart about the law?" Trace said. "You'll still be an accomplice."

"I'll claim you abducted me. I was just at a little convention and you made me come with you. You said if I didn't come with you, you'd take it out on poor Mr. Nishimoto."

Trace pushed the front door open and called inside, "Anybody to home?"

There was no answer.

"Yoohoo. It's the Welcome Wagon. Anybody to home?"

"Nobody's to home," he told Chico as they went inside.

The front door opened directly into a small living room, which was easily the messiest room Trace had ever seen. Newspapers were strewn everywhere. Half-filled coffeecups sat on end tables, corroding. A single ashtray was overflowing with cigarette butts. Dust balls were clumped in the corners, the couch cushions were askew; the rear windows through which the afternoon sun shone dimly looked as if they had never been washed.

"Take a good look, Trace," Chico said. "This is how you'll be living if I ever decide to move out."

"Not bloody likely," he said. "I'll get me another neat roommate."

"Dog," she said.

To the right of the living room were two small bedrooms; the door to the left opened into a large eat-in kitchen, with a bathroom in the far corner.

The kitchen was just as dirty as the living room. Dishes were piled in the sink and on the table. Pots on the stove looked as if they had been used repeatedly but never washed.

Chico took a sponge, wet it under the faucet, and began wiping as she walked around the room.

Trace went back to the living room. Behind him, he heard Chico grumbling that there wasn't much food in the house. Then she poked her head into the doorway between the rooms.

"Are you getting hungry?" she asked.

"Are you hungry again?"

"I haven't eaten since . . ."

"Since lunch. Two hours ago. Don't you ever stop?" he asked.

"Maybe just a nibble. Think he'd mind if I cooked up something?"

"No. What the hell. We're looking for him. If he shows up, he'll have more to talk about than the fact that you killed off his last can of pork and beans."

"Good thinking, Trace."

Trace looked through the dirty rear windows out over the land. He saw the small utility shed to the left and then the trees growing, from wherever the seeds fell, over the property. There were no fences and no indication where this property stopped and the next owner's land began.

The only two houses visible were widely separated and at least five hundred yards away.

Trace thought the living room looked like a roach motel, only not so neat. There could have been a body buried under all those newspapers, for all he knew.

He pushed things aside, straightening up a little as he went, but found nothing under the surface layer dirt and disorder other than old newspapers and magazines.

The first bedroom's bed was unmade. The closet held only a single pair of jeans, man's size Calvin Kleins, Trace noticed with disgust. The dresser was empty except for some men's underwear and a few basic gray sweatshirts.

The other bedroom had been set up as a

small office. There was a plain wooden desk, small, the type often used in children's rooms. Atop it was a telephone that worked. Inside the desk drawers, he found only usual office supplies, ballpoint pens, pads, a stapler, a box of paper clips, four real-estate manuals.

In the back of the desk, underneath a newspaper, he found a Rolodex and he flipped it open to the Ms. No Mandy. He carefully went through all the listings, but there were only about two dozen names, all of them apparently real-estate brokers and attorneys and all strictly business.

It looked, simply, like an office away from home for Thomas Collins. Yet something seemed missing, though Trace couldn't remember what.

He went back into the living room and heard Chico puttering around the kitchen, humming softly. She always seemed happiest, Trace thought, when eating or preparing food. If she developed enough good karma, when she came back in the next life, she might come back as a praying mantis, consuming ten times her own weight in food every day and eating nonstop from morning till night.

Being a woman was a pretty good deal, all in all, he thought. Just worry about food and ignore the really big questions of truth, justice, budget deficits, and morality. Maybe when he came back he would come back as a woman.

Maybe his ex-wife would too, he thought.

"Lunch will be ready in a minute," Chico called.

"You're not making a mess in that kitchen, are you?"

"You'll never recognize the place," he heard her say.

The hot tub. That's what it was. The note from Mandy had mentioned the hot tub at the farm, but where was there room for a hot tub in this mess?

He opened the door from the living room to the rear of the house and found the redwood tub off on the side, built into a little platform and surrounded by high shrubbery. In the east, they tended to use fiberglass; in California, nothing but a big organic tub out of organic wood would do. The tub was sealed off with a wooden cover like an oversized sewer plate. He slid it aside. The water was still and clear and, when he dipped a finger into it, cold.

He found the controls in a weatherproof circuit box alongside a bench on the small platform and turned the tub on. It started immediately to whoosh heavy streams of water from three different outlets inside the tub, and Trace thought, What the hell, why not?

Back inside, he roared, "Woman, is there any vodka in this house?"

"How would I know? I'm into stealing food, not liquor."

After fruitlessly searching the cabinets and getting in Chico's way, Trace found the liquor hidden under the sink. Another mark against

Thomas Collins. Liquor should be displayed proudly, as a totem of the civilized man leading the civilized life. People who put liquor under the sink were dirty little pernicious drinkers who thought of alcohol as something basically shameful. Drano belonged under the sink; liquor belonged on the counter, in full view.

Strike two against Thomas Collins. He had no vodka. He had a bottle of cheap rum, cheaper Scotch, and rye that was so off-brand that Trace was surprised it was still brown.

He started on the Scotch, mixing it with water from the tap and adding a few ice cubes from the tiny old refrigerator's freezer tray, which was barely large enough to hold a carton of cigarettes.

The kitchen was already on its way to clean. The worst of the litter had been moved aside; dishes were stacked neatly on the sink, and the small kitchen table had been washed clean and set with two plates, silverware, and paper napkins. Chico had used paper towels for placemats. There was a bowl of something green and steamy in the center of the table.

"Sit and eat," Chico said as she sat down. "I'm starving. Cooking always makes me hungry."

He sat facing her, Scotch in hand, and watched unenthusiastically as she put some of the food onto his plate. She drank from a large glass of water, as she always did with meals.

"Yum, yum," Trace said. "What is this gruel?"

"It's a special Japanese dish," she said.

"Where's the raw fish?"

"No raw fish. This is reftovers. Chicken bits and frozen vegetables, all in a special sauce of my own design."

"I can't eat this slop," he said.

"Good. More for me."

He ate a few forkfuls of the food, finished his drink, and went to the counter to make another. When he turned back, Chico had switched plates and was eating his food. Her empty plate was in front of his seat.

"I figured you were done," she mumbled through a full mouth.

He leaned against the sink and watched her eat. It was like watching time lapse photography—thousands of years compressed into a few seconds—of something like the Colorado River cutting through hundreds of feet of rock to create the Grand Canyon. There was something equally inexorable about Chico eating. It was like a force of nature.

"You eat like somebody who grew up with fourteen siblings," he said.

She mumbled agreement.

"In a poverty ward," he said.

She nodded agreeably, chewing all the while.

"If Dickens had known you, he would have written a book about you. You'd be a star. You'd have a TV movie. *The Thing That Ate the World*."

She finally gulped and swallowed and stood up. "Get out of here and go play detective. I want to do these dishes."

The water in the hot tub had already warmed perceptibly, so Trace took his clothes off, tossed them in a pile on the small bench near the tub, and sat in the warming water. He reached over and hit one of the switches inside the junction box and the aerator started bubbling hot water up through jets in the bottom of the tub. The motor pumping the air-water mix sounded like a vacuum cleaner sucking tacks. It wasn't long until Chico came out of the house looking for the source of the sound.

She pushed her head between bushes and saw him in the tub.

"Come on in, the water's fine," he said.

"Well, aren't you a perv?" she said.

"You already knew that. Come on in."

She snatched the Scotch glass from his hand and walked away. When she came back onto the deck a few minutes later, she was naked, holding a fresh drink in her hand.

"The way I like you best," Trace said as Chico handed him the glass and slid down beneath the bubbling warm waters. "Without clothes and without pretensions, serving your man."

"You wish," she said. "I hope this guy doesn't have herpes."

"Trust you to find a way to ruin this romantic moment," Trace said.

"Vell now, Mr. Tracy, now zat you are relaxed here at Ze Touchie-Feelie California Therapy Institute, suppose you tell me vot iss der problem?" Chico said.

"I'm perfectly normal."

"The first rule of Ze Touchie-Feelie Therapy Institute is dot no vun iss perfectly normal. Everybody iss a sickie. Ozervise vy did God invent California? Vy are you not married?"

"I was married but it didn't work."

"Vy not?"

"My wife wanted me to sleep with her."

"And you don't like sex?"

"I didn't like my wife," Trace said. "She had this disconcerting habit of getting pregnant."

"So you haff children?"

"Ach. I mean, yes. Two children, What's-his-name and the girl."

"What is your relationship with them?"

"It's very good," Trace said.

"Tell me about it."

"I haven't seen them in four years."

"How can you consider dat a good relationship?"

"How can you consider it anything less than perfect?" Trace asked.

"And your life since divorcing them all has been happy?"

"No, it's been miserable," Trace said. "I went from accountant to gambler and from gambles to addict. You see, I got hooked on this crazed Eurasian woman who is sapping my vital juices. And if that's not degrading enough,

I have to fence at least three stolen televisions a day just to keep her in food."

"Der diagnosis iss very clear," Chico said. "Very clear indeed."

"Yes? What can I do, Doctor?"

"Have you ever heard of taking the pipe?" Chico said.

"You know, Chico, you're better than most therapists. You've recommended suicide in just the first visit. Think of all the money you'd save your patients."

"We aim to please," she said. She looked up at a flock of birds that were noisily flapping their way overhead. A soft breeze rustled through the shrubbery surrounding the hot tub. "You really do feel sorry for yourself, don't you?" she said.

"I feel sorrier for other people."

"Like who?"

"Women bodybuilders," Trace said.

"How's that?"

"They all start bodybuilding to make their tits bigger, and when they're done, they've got big ugly biceps and they still don't have any tits. Now that's worth feeling sorry for. That, and an empty glass." He showed her his glass, stood up in the tub, and walked wet-footed into the house.

11

Dressed again, Chico was sitting on the sofa, idly thumbing through a pile of magazines and newspapers on the dingy old coffee table.

"Hey, Trace," she said. "You want to get your pipes cleaned?"

"This isn't even my house," Trace said.

"Tell that to Monica. She's got an ad in here for cleaning your pipes and hauling your ashes."

She turned a page and Trace was able to see that she was reading a sex tabloid that had been on the table under the pile of magazines. "Hey, here's one if you want to get off over the phone."

"I wouldn't do that," Trace said.

"Why not?"

"It leaves the phone sticky for the next person," Trace said. "I'm going out to the barn."

Trace looked through a window into the small utility building behind the house. There was no tractor. A few tools were hung on the far wall, opposite the window. A large pile of leaf cuttings and grass cuttings occupied the middle of the floor.

Trace removed the locking pin, and the shed's wooden door, twice the size of a regular house door, swung open easily and quietly.

A sharp smell jumped from the building into his nose, and for a moment he gagged and turned away. He had an idea what the smell was because, once smelled, it was never forgotten.

He took a deep breath of fresh outside air, cleared his lungs, then took another deep breath, held it, and went back inside to the pile of grass on the floor. He touched it with the toe of his shoe and moved some of it aside. He pushed his foot farther and his toe hit something unyielding. He kicked the grass aside and saw a man's trouser leg.

Trace went outside to breathe again, held another deep breath, went back inside, and used his shoe to move the grass away.

A dead man was under the pile of grass, lying on his back, blackened dried blood caked along the side of his head. He was wearing a white shirt, jeans, and ornately tooled cowboy boots. His thinning white hair was too long and stood out in poofs on both sides of his neck. It was Thomas Collins.

Trace turned when he heard a sound behind him and saw Chico at the doorway to the barn. He hurried until he was outside in the fresh air and gasped deeply.

Chico looked at him questioningly.

"You don't want to go in there," he said.

"Why not? What's the smell?" she asked. She was holding her tabloid newspaper in her hand.

"It's Thomas Collins."

"What's he wearing?" Chico asked.

"Mostly flies and maggots. What do you mean what's he wearing?"

"How did he die? Can you tell?"

"The side of his head is laid open," Trace said. "I think he got clubbed."

"Maybe a fall? Maybe he hit his head?" she offered.

"I didn't get a real chance to look around, but I don't think so. It doesn't look like there's anything in there to hit your head on."

"I guess we should call the police," Chico said.

"Let's not rush into things," said Trace. He closed the barn door but did not relock it. He saw Chico shaking her head.

"Trust you," she said. "I take you away on vacation and what is it, another murder. I'm getting tired of being involved in murders every time I go anywhere with you."

"I think it's getting old myself," Trace said. "All I want to do is go back to San Francisco and get the next lecture on The Future of Japanese Life Insurance in a Changing World. Why do you have that paper?"

"Oh." She handed it to Trace. An advertisement was circled with red magic marker. It read: "Live out your sexual fantasies. Spend a night with Mandy." It gave a San Francisco telephone number.

"Why'd you circle it in red?" Trace asked.

"I didn't," Chico said. "It was circled when I found it."

Trace dialed the number in San Francisco.

A woman answered, her voice soft and breathy.

"Hello. I hope I can do something for you."

"Hello," Trace said. "This is Thomas Collins." He stopped and waited.

Finally the woman said, "And?"

"Is this Mandy?"

"Yes, it is."

"This is Thomas Collins," Trace said again.

The woman chuckled. "I don't need your name, honey. Just your bank balance. What can I do for you?"

"I wanted to tell you that I got the cuff link back."

"Cuff link? What cuff link?"

"The one you sent me," Trace said.

"Listen, Mr. Collins, or whatever your name is, I didn't send you any cuff link. Now do you want something with me?"

"I'm sorry, Mandy. I thought you were the girl who spent the night at my farm out near Nicasio."

"Wrong girl, but it sounds like a wonderful idea," she said. "Especially if you have a hayloft." She laughed again and Trace thought she had a wonderful sexy, throaty laugh.

"I'll give you a call later," he said.

"Sure, honey, you do that," she said, her voice sounding disbelieving. "You just call anytime."

Trace hung up and turned away from the telephone. It had probably not been smart to call because now there would be a record on Collins' telephone of the phone call to Mandy, but it had seemed right at the time.

Chico had been watching him from the bedroom doorway. "Well?" she said.

"I think we got the wrong Mandy," he said.

"Are you going to call the police now?"

"I don't know. I think I'd like to just not get involved," Trace said. "Just get out of here and let somebody else find the body some other time."

"You're still going to wind up involved in it," Chico said. "When the body's found, somebody'll talk to Mrs. Collins and she'll mention your name and they'll be all over you. There's no hiding, Trace."

"Christ, you're depressing to talk to," he said.

"I just went out to the barn."

"You didn't have to do that."

"Yes, I did. I wanted to see what the body was wearing," Chico said.

"So what was he wearing?"

"One cuff link," Chico said.

"I guess it is Collins, then, isn't it? I was hoping it might be somebody else."

"No, it's him," Chico said. "I checked his wallet. His driver's license is in there."

"Anything else?"

"Credit cards, business cards, a few dollars, but nothing personal. No telephone numbers or anything," she said. "I think I found the murder weapon too."

Trace looked up from the small desk and Chico nodded. "There's a bloody baseball bat out behind the barn," she said.

"What a pain in the ass you are," Trace said.

"I know. Call the police."

"Maybe later," he said.

12

Trace went back out the small barn, opened the door, took a deep breath, then went inside and kicked the grass back over Collins' body.

He relocked the door, then found the bloody baseball bat in tall grass behind the small outbuilding. It was a short, narrow bat, with a six-inch smear of lumpy, fleshy darkened bloodstain over the bat's label. Bad batting form, he thought.

When he went back inside, he asked Chico, "Did you touch the bat?"

"No. I didn't want to leave prints."

"Good. What are you doing?"

"I don't want to leave prints in here either," she said. "I'm cleaning up."

Trace looked around the kitchen and was convinced that the room had not been that clean since the first day the little house was built. Dishes were stacked neatly on the sink, the table and counters had been cleaned, and now Chico was sweeping the floor.

"I don't remember your getting fingerprints on the floor," he said.

"You can't be too careful. I don't want to be blamed for murder," she said.

"Quit being dramatic, Chico. You've scrubbed every surface in the room. No self-respecting fingerprint would dare to show up here."

"Don't get smart. There's a witness, you know," she said.

"Who?"

"That looney we stopped for directions," she said. "With our luck he'll have his first lucid moment in forty years, and he'll give the cops our description and our license plate. We'll rot in jail until our skins turn the color of fish bellies."

"It'll all be your fault," Trace said. "If you hadn't insisted on your hourly feeding, we could have come and gone, and none the wiser. If the cops find us now, it'll be because the kitchen's too clean. They'll take one look and know the Beige Peril was here with her killer dishrag."

She brushed by him into the living room, cleaning cloth in hand. He took the occasion to make another drink, but because he knew she'd ask questions, he wiped the faucet and the Scotch bottle and he carried the glass wrapped inside a paper towel.

In the living room, she had straightened up the piles of papers and magazines and was wiping off the coffee table.

"Go wipe off the controls for that hot tub," she said.

He did as ordered. When he came back inside, Chico was in the bedroom and called him in.

"Notice anything?" she said.

"Give me a clue."

"Those dirty curtains," she said.

"You're not doing laundry and that's all there is to it," Trace said flatly.

"No. Come over here and take a whiff."

"I've given up curtain sniffing. Bicycle seats are so much more rewarding," Trace said.

He walked over and she guided his head toward the ruffle at the bottom of the curtain.

"Don't you notice anything?" she said, gripping his neck with her tiny steel-hard fingers. "It's a smell. Do you smell it?"

"No," he said. "All the blood in my body has rushed to my head. I'm too busy trying to remain conscious to smell anything."

"Anyone with a nose that wasn't deadened by twenty years of vodka fumes could smell it," she said.

"Smell what?"

"Evening in Byzantium, fool." She pushed him aside and dropped to her knees near the window.

"What does Byzantium have to do with anything?" Trace said. "And why are you on your knees paying homage to Collins' bedroom wall."

"Evening in Byzantium is a perfume," she

said. "Patchouli, cinnamon, lemon grass, a hint of tuberose, and a metallic high note," she said.

"That's terrific, Chico. When you're finished dealing blackjack, maybe you can hire out to the Canine Corps to sniff out explosives."

"The nose doesn't lie," she said. "Here." She pointed to the floor and Trace dropped down beside her. He followed her finger and saw a few slivers of glass embedded in the shabby worn carpeting

"Good," he said. "You don't think Collins was beaten to death with a perfume bottle, do you? What about the baseball bat?"

"You're the big detective, not me," she said. "You're supposed to figure things out. All I know is that somebody smashed a bottle of expensive perfume against this wall."

"The glass is gone, though," Trace said.

"Would you leave glass on your bedroom floor? Well, you might, but most people wouldn't. I saw some glass in the garbage bag in the kitchen."

Trace shrugged. "It might have happened months ago."

"No. It was recent. The fragrance would have vanished after a couple of weeks," she said.

"If you say so," Trace said. "Now if Chico Chan has finished looking for clues, I'd like to get out of here."

"You still don't want to call the police?"

"Now less than ever," Trace said.

13

Back at the hotel on the fringes of the city's Chinatown, Trace removed the tape recorder from under his shirt while Chico talked to her mother in the next room.

Trace took a shower to get the sticky tape residue off his side, and when he came out, Chico was sitting in a chair looking out the window.

"We've got a problem," she said.

"What's that?" he asked. He was wrapped in a towel and he took clean underwear from the dresser drawer.

"My mother. Mr. Nishimoto tried to put the make on her."

"I think Emmie can handle herself," Trace said.

"That's just it. He made a lunge for her at the cocktail hour this afternoon and she threw her orange juice at him."

"Not a bad maneuver," Trace said, slipping into his Jockey shorts.

"But now she feels so bad about embarrassing him that she thinks she's going to kill herself. She's trying to figure out now how to do it."

"The only difference between your mother and mine," Trace said, "is that your mother threatens suicide four times a day. I thought you'd be used to it by now."

"That's not the only difference," Chico said. "My mother's nice."

Trace nodded. "That's true," he said. "And she's little. My mother looks like a piece of earthmoving equipment."

"I think you should talk to my mother," Chico said.

"About what?"

"Tell her what she did isn't so bad."

"Will it make you feel better?" Trace said.

"Me and her," Chico said.

"Will you sleep with me then?"

"I'll give it serious consideration," Chico said.

"Serious consideration yes or serious consideration no?"

"Serious consideration maybe," Chico said.

"I haven't had any better offers today," Trace said.

They found Chico's mother sitting beneath a banana tree in the hotel lobby. She was scribbling into a notebook.

"Hi, Emmie," Trace said. "What's up?" He sat next to her on a small sofa. Chico sat on a chair facing them across the small cocktail table.

"Hello, You," Emmie said. "I write poem." She added cheerfully, "Death poem."

"What for?" Trace asked.

"It is for leave behind." She showed him the notebook page covered with Japanese characters. "But it is unworthy," she said. The smile of her face turned upside down. "Mr. Nishimoto will feel shame to receive it and then I not able to kill myself again for second shaming."

"One to a customer, that's what they always say," Trace said. He looked up to see Chico glaring at him.

"You see, You, I do terrible thing to Mr. Nishimoto. I shame him in front of whole convention. Such requires great death poem."

Trace gently took the notebook from her and put it on the cocktail table, then held her hands in his.

"Maybe in Japan, Emmie, but not here. I happen to know for a fact that Mr. Nishimoto doesn't rate a death poem, never mind a death."

Mrs. Mangini's eyes widened in surprise. "No? Why no, You?"

"Because I once tried the same thing with a woman that he tried with you."

"You did?"

He nodded. "Right in the Araby Casino, it was. A Japanese woman too. Well, part Japanese anyway."

"Did she shame you?" Chico's mother asked, her eyebrows raised in question.

"She did more than shame me. She punched me with her pointy little fists."

"And she did not commit suicide?"

"No," Trace said solemnly. "She promised, though, that she would spend the rest of *her* life making *my* life miserable."

"Shameless," Mrs. Mangini said. "She should have taken own life."

"No, not in America. That's what I'm saying, Emmie. In America, you don't do that anymore. Not for orange juice anyway. I mean, it wasn't like you wasted a real drink."

"Aha," Chico's mother said. "I begin to understand. Suicide not required for all beverages in this country."

"Absolutely not. You're a free woman, Emmie."

She squeezed his hand. "I am happy, You," she said. "But what of woman who shamed you? What of her?"

Chico interrupted before Trace could speak. "He got even, Mother. He has spent all the years since then shaming her." She glared at Trace.

Mrs. Mangini shook her head. "You Americans are very complicated. Suicide seem much easier."

"Not in America," Trace said. "Trust me."

"I trust you, You. I happy now. Come. We go to movie together in great happiness."

Before Trace could decline, Chico accepted

for both of them. "Trace loves Japanese movies. We'd love to come."

"Why'd you say that?" Trace whispered as they walked to the room where the movie was being shown. "I hate Japanese movies. Everybody's always barking at everybody else."

"Part of my lifelong plan to make your life miserable," Chico said sweetly.

The movie was already in progress. Dozens of men in kimonos, faces painted white, slashed at one another on the screen while the audience sat watching in appreciative silence.

"What's the name of this?" Trace whispered.

The Eighteen Samurai," Chico said. "It's the eleventh in a series that began with *The Seven Samurai.*"

"At least we didn't have to see the first ten," Trace said.

"Don't worry. There are thirty-one more," Chico said.

Trace fidgeted in his seat. The film had no subtitles, obviously because everyone in the place except Trace spoke Japanese.

"How do you tell the characters apart?" he asked. "They all look the same."

"How do you tell Alec Guinness from Prince?" Chico snapped back at him.

"That's easy. Prince wears leopard underwear. What I don't understand is why is everybody so quiet."

"You mean, besides you," Chico said.

"Right. We've seen five characters get their heads lopped off and not so much as a whistle. You think they'd be glad or sad or something. Do you think everybody in here is asleep?"

"No," Chico said. "The Japanese are educated not to show their emotions. Public displays of emotion are only for barbarians like you."

"Oh." Trace thought about it for a moment. "Like the emotionless way you're always abusing me."

Chico snorted.

"Well, I don't believe it," Trace said. "I think most of these people don't know what's going on here any more than I do. They're just being polite, sitting here, biding their time until they can go to the bar and get a drink. That's what I think." He stood up.

"What are you doing?" Chico asked.

"I'm going to beat the rush to the bar."

Two Finlandias later, the eighteen unidentifiable samurai had become no more than a horrible dream, but the memory of Thomas Collins' maggot-ridden body was still too clear. He had been murdered, and his murderer was walking around free.

Trace didn't want to get involved. This case had nothing to do with him, and in truth from everything he'd heard, he would not have liked Thomas Collins, scuzzbag, very much at all.

But getting away with killing went against his grain.

He called Mrs. Collins from a pay phone in the cocktail lounge.

"Have you found out anything yet?" she asked. Her voice sounded strained, as if she'd been waiting by the phone all day for some word on her husband.

Trace had called with the intention of telling her where—and in what condition—he had found her husband, but when he heard her voice, something pulled him up short.

"I'm still looking into things," he said. "But I still think you should call the police and report your husband missing."

"Oh, but I can't . . ." Her voice trailed off miserably.

"It's been a week. That's long enough for anyone to get worried. He's not going to be mad at you." Trace thought of Thomas Collins lying in the barn with his skull crushed. "I'm sure he won't be angry. And you did say you'd call the police."

"Well, perhaps, if you really think I ought to."

"That's what I think," Trace said.

"If I do, will you keep looking for him all the same?" she asked timidly.

Trace knew when he was beaten. "Yeah, I will," he said. "No one's heard anything from him? Not even your daughter?"

"No, I spoke to Tammy last night. She didn't mention Thomas at all."

"Thanks a lot, Mrs. Collins. Call the police."

Trace hung up before he got into any more losing negotiations.

Trace clicked the receiver, then called Michael Mabley's office and repeated the same dismal no-progress report.

"That's too bad," Mabley said. There was a disappointed accusation in his voice that annoyed Trace. Even Mabley's disembodied voice rubbed him the wrong way.

"That's the way it goes sometimes," Trace said. "I told Mrs. Collins to call the cops."

"I guess that's best. There was a story in the paper today that you might be interested in."

"It wasn't on the sports page, I guess," said Trace. "I only read the sports pages."

"No. It was in the business news. It said that Collins and Rose pulled out as sponsoring developers of a shopping mall near the Presidio."

"What does that mean?" Trace asked. "I won't understand business until they can condense it into box scores."

"What it might very well mean is that Collins and Rose are in deep financial trouble. Newspapers never give you the details in cases like that, but that's what it could mean. Collins and Rose overextended themselves and they're capital-short."

"You think it has something to do with Collins being missing?" Trace said.

"*You're* the detective. But maybe Collins took the gas pipe or something."

"Hope so," Trace advised. "Then we won't have to pay off on the insurance policy." Maybe Mabley wasn't such a creep at all, Trace thought. "Thanks for keeping your eyes open," he said.

"Just trying to lend a hand to Gone Fishing's best man," Mabley said with a chuckle that made Trace dislike him all over again.

14

Trace's Log: Tuesday night, Tape Number One in the Thomas Collins matter. I taunted God and lost.

What I did was pack this damned tape recorder and God saw me and he said, Oho, oho, if Trace is stupid enough to pack that damned tape recorder, then let's make sure he gets to use it.

And now look at me. I've broken the damned law by not reporting a body that we found; I'm wasting my time at a convention by working; the worst of all, I'm forced into repeated contact with some creature who seems to be proud of being a friend of Walter Marks.

This is no fair, God, and I want you to know I'll be keeping score from now on. Maybe you can get away with that short-end-of-the-stick stuff with Job, but not with me.

I'm not too worried about breaking the law. I think I can blame that on Chico. If the cops come, I'll just tell them, Sure, I was out at the

farm with her, just to poach my impurities in
the hot tub. But you'd better check the dead
guy's wallet and stuff, I bet her fingerprints
are all over it. And if that doesn't work, I'll
break one of her bottles of Evening in Byzantium and give the cops the pieces and tell
them to snort the bedroom drapes. Chico can
fry, as far as I'm concerned. That's what she
gets for talking me into coming to this lunatic
bin, to watch samurai movies and keep an eye
on Mr. Nishimoto, the man of the wandering
hands. And make sure that Emmie doesn't
commit suicide. No sense dying over spilled
orange juice.

Why me, God? I don't know, Trace.

Thank you, Groucho, for giving me Mike
Mabley. Junk jewelry, Gucci loafers, little
galoshes in his smelly new car to protect his
little shoesies. And a grateful pat on the back
to Mabley for involving me with Mrs. Collins,
alias the Mud Fence. I've heard of henpecked,
but what is she? Cock-pecked? I've got a good
suspicion that Tom Collins—that's right, the
bastard is dead and I'm going to call him
Tom whether he liked it or not—anyway, I've
got a good suspicion that Tom Collins is
a—check that was—a grade-A wife-beater.

And he owned a farm that his wife didn't
even know about, so let that answer the question of whether he was out tipping on his wife
or not. He was. At least once with Laurie
Anders, the resident beauty of the Collins-Rose

real-estate agency, and with everybody else in town to hear Laurie and Rafe Rose tell of it.

More proof. The cuff link. Don't laugh, big guy, it's our hottest clue so far. We've got a cuff link sent to Collins' postal box along with a neatly printed note signed Mandy. Add to that a classified ad in some handjob newspaper for a hooker named Mandy who didn't know what I was talking about.

Point Two. So Collins' body is at the farm, but where's his car?

Point. I'd call this Point Three but I don't think there was ever a Point One. Anyway, point, Chico's nose—a deadly weapon honed on years of sniffing out food supplies—says that somebody broke a bottle of perfume in Collins' bedroom at the farm recently. Why?

Who knows?

Who cares?

The only reason I'm involved in this at all is because of that deformed midget prick, Walter Marks, and now I'm just worried that when the body gets found, the cops'll talk to Mrs. Collins and she'll hand me up on a melamine platter.

Point some number or other. Mabley found an item in the paper that says the real-estate agency pulled out of a deal and that might mean they're short on money. Rafe Rose didn't seem exactly crushed by the thought of Collins being among the missing. Maybe it's bad enough that Rose does most of the real-estate work and has to give fifty percent to Collins but if Collins is going south with money that belongs to the firm, Rose could get ticked enough to line-drive Collins' skull with a baseball bat.

Laurie Anders can't stand Collins. And neither can his wife, who stands to gain two hundred thou from his insurance policy. And then there's the stepdaughter, Tammy, at Hollyhope College who, according to Laurie, hated Collins, too. Well, why not? I hate him myself for doing this to me.

And then there's Mandy, the hooker. People in her line of work have been known to stretch the truth now and then. Maybe a personal visit is in order, if I can convince Chico that it's strictly in the line of duty.

Nice way for a decent well-intentioned young man to spend his vacation, huh? I am not real happy with this turn of events, God, and if I were you, I'd look over my shoulder once in a while because you're on my list.

My costs, thank you, Mr. Walter Marks, have been phenomenally high and much too elaborate to itemize. Know ye, therefore, that my bill so far is one thousand dollars, and that's just in expenses. I'm sure more will come to mind as time goes on.

No, hold that. Expenses will drop dramatically tomorrow. I'm posting a sign on the hotel bulletin board: My consort, Michiko Mangini, having left my bed and board, will now be held solely responsible for any food bills incurred by her.

Hell, that'd take care of the national deficit.

Come to think of it, Mandy sounds better than ever.

Good night, world. And God, if you're listening, phhhht to you."

15

Trace woke up with a ringing in his ears. There was only one reasonable explanation: the Vienna Choirboys' hand-bell chorus was practicing in his head. Again. And they were all wearing golf shoes.

He groaned. At least his throat still worked well enough to produce some semihuman sounds.

"Eat these," Chico said. She was sitting on the edge of the bed and she forced two aspirins into the parched slot of his mouth. Then she hoisted up his head and poured water into it from a glass. When she released his head, it dropped back onto the pillow like an cannonball.

He groaned again.

"Feel that bad, huh?" she said.

"It's that water. I hate water. It dilutes all the vital fluids in your body."

"The only fluid in your body is alcohol," Chico said. "You've heard, 'my blood ran cold'?

Well, yours runs clear. Maybe that was how the Egyptians made mummies. Tank up people with vodka and keep them pickled for five thousand years. Sit up. I've ordered breakfast."

"Can't sit," Trace said. He felt the aspirins dissolving on his tongue. The water flow had somehow missed them. "I hear bells. It's the end. St. Peter's calling me."

"Those are bells from some church down the block," Chico said. "Walter Marks called. He wants you to get back to him as soon as you wake up."

"Screw him. This is all his fault. I'm never talking to him again. Screw him."

"No, thanks. But he is your boss."

"Just another one of God's tests on my patience," Trace said.

The room-service waiter came while Trace was still in bed. Chico had him wheel a table laden with enough food for a Boy Scout troop over near the window, then dismissed him with a large cash tip that she took from Trace's wallet.

"When you use my money, undertip," Trace told her. "I can't eat all that."

"Who says you have to?" She tossed him a roll. He tried to catch it, missed, and the roll hit him between the eyes. "That's for you," she said. "That and two sausages. The rest is mine. You like sausages, don't you?"

"No," Trace said.

"Good. More for me." Chico sat at the table and started on the platters of french toast,

omelets, bacon, sausage, and pastries, complaining bitterly that the hotel offered only
apple and cherry marmalades with the toast.
"No grape jelly anywhere," she said.

"God, you're disgusting."

"I'm fortifying myself," she said. "It'll be a
long drive to Hollyhope College today. I looked
it up on the map in the lobby and we'll be on
the road a couple of hours. I know how crabby
you get about having to stop for food while
you're driving."

"Correction," Trace said. "*I'll* be on the
road. You'll be here, watching *The Twenty-
Seven Samurai* with your mother. Anyway, how
did you know about Hollyhope College?"

"I listened to your log this morning," Chico
said.

Trace sat up in bed. "I keep telling you
those tapes are personal. My property. Hands
off. Don't you have any ethics at all?"

Chico stopped eating for the briefest of mo-
ments. "I don't think so," she said. "Seeing
Tammy Collins is a good idea, but Mandy the
Hooker doesn't sound like much of a lead to
me."

"I'll be the judge of that, if you don't mind,"
Trace said. "I'm the investigator here, surprising as that may be to you."

"I'm not surprised," she said, licking her
fingers. "You've probably logged more hours
investigating types like Mandy than any detective west of the Mississippi."

"Jealousy rears its sausage-filled head,"

Trace said. He tried to get up out of the bed. "And I'm not a detective," he said.

"What are you?"

"What I am, Chico, is, God help me, a man with a hangover. I don't get hangovers, but here, I think I've got one."

"I'm sorry, Trace," Chico said earnestly. "I know what this means to your drinking career."

"Don't joke. This is serious. If I'm going to get hangovers, how can I drink so much?"

"Maybe God is sending you a message to slow down," she suggested.

"It must be Get Devlin Tracy Week in heaven," Trace said. "Why doesn't God just butt out? Hasn't he done enough?"

"I don't know about your problems with God," she said. "Here's a deal," she said as she got up and stole the breakfast roll from Trace's bed. "You can see Mandy if you want, but I go along to Hollyhope College. Okay?" She demolished the roll.

"All right," he relented. "But since you've eaten everything, we'll have to stop somewhere along the way for a sandwich."

"That's okay with me," Chico said. "I'm starving."

16

Tammy Collins lived in an apartment above a gymnasium called the Body Eternal. The building was painted in Day-Glo purple, adorned with white silhouettes of impossibly endowed men and women.

When they opened the ground-level door, a smell hit them, as bad in its way as the smell from Thomas Collins' barn.

Chico wrinkled up her nose. "B.O.," she sang.

"Stuff cotton in your delicate Oriental nostrils," Trace said. "You were the one who insisted on coming along."

He led the way up the stairs, past the door to the gym on the right, to the second-floor landing. He knocked.

He thought the smell would be less pungent up here, but as the apartment door swung open, even Trace's jaded smeller cringed in front of the ripe odor of sweating bodies, although he did his best to ignore it.

The young woman who stood before him

would have been a beauty anywhere, but it seemed that she was taking both makeup and fashion lessons from her mother. She wore no makeup, her hair was uncombed, and she was wearing a shapeless caftan. She was not perspiring at all. Her eyes were her only live feature, displaying open and vibrant hostility.

Trace introduced himself and Chico.

"I know who you are," Tammy Collins said with sullen recognition. "My mother warned me that you might come up here."

"Has she called the police yet?" Trace asked.

Tammy shrugged. "I hope not. She ought to give him a chance."

"A chance to do what?" Trace asked.

"To be dead." She smiled, showing off perfectly formed, pearl-white teeth. "You don't have to tell me what you're thinking. The girl hated her stepfather, right, Sherlock?"

"Right, Lucretia," Trace said.

"Touché. You specialize in sarcasm too?"

"Only when I'm hung over. I wanted to talk to you about your stepfather."

"You're wasting your time," the young woman said, "but come on in anyway." She waved them to a couch that was so stained and dirty that simultaneously, without consultation, both Trace and Chico decided they'd rather stand.

The smell was just as bad inside the apartment, now that the door was closed.

"You're wasting your time, Hawkshaw. I

haven't talked to Daddy Dearest in months. Not since school started. And damn little before that, if I could get away with it."

From an adjoining room came a grunt and then the deep thump of something heavy being set down.

"What's that?" Trace asked.

"Just Julio, the guy I live with. Want to meet him?"

"I'll pass," Chico said, sniffing the air.

Trace pinched her surreptitiously and said, "We'd rather talk to you. Unless Julio knows something."

Into the room walked a young man wearing bathing trunks and a wide leather weight lifter's belt. He was the shortiest ugliest sweatiest person Trace had ever seen, except for Walter Marks. And possibly Trace's ex-wife.

"That's Julio?" Trace said.

Tammy nodded and Trace said, "Julio doesn't know anything."

"Julio Hernández, meet Dick Tracy," Tammy said smugly.

"I don't like flatfoots," Julio growled.

"That's flatfeet, stinkbomb," Trace said mildly.

Julio moved forward menacingly, like an ambulatory haymow, one quivering muscle at a time. Trace moved away from the windowsill where he'd been leaning, but Chico stepped in between them and stood in front of Julio.

"You've got the best trapeziuses I ever saw. How do you do that?"

"Shrugs," he said. "Heavyweight shrugs." He crouched over like the Incredible Hulk so the trapezius muscles between neck and shoulder bunched up. Trace was forgotten as Julio concentrated on the really important thing in his life: his own body and what people thought of it.

"I'd love to see your equipment," Chico said.

Julio snickered. "Come on inside," he said.

Trace tossed a dirty look Chico's way as she led the squat young man gently out of the room.

"Notice," he said. "From the rear they form the number ten."

"More power to her," Tammy said. "Most people can't control him. She probably saved your life."

"I doubt it," Trace said. "The dumber they are, the harder they fall. What's he majoring in? Jock itch?"

"Oh, Julio doesn't go to school. He's training to be Mister Universe. That's why we live here. It's the only place in town that'll let him keep barbells."

"Why doesn't he use the gym downstairs?" Trace asked.

"Julio likes to use his own equipment," Tammy said. She sprawled back on the couch, showing a lot of very nice left leg from under her caftan. "What's his is his."

"Including you?"

The young woman stiffened. "I thought you came here to talk about my stepfather."

"All right. Maybe you can start by telling me why you hate him."

She exhaled slowly. "That would take more years than you've got left."

"Just hit the high spots," Trace said.

"Is rape high enough?"

"He raped you?" Trace asked.

"He tried, the scumbag. Just this past summer. We were alone in the house. Mother was out with that stupid Artisans' Guild trying to sell some of her work. She has to pay my tuition herself. Anyway, he gave me a drink. It was the first nice thing he ever did. I said thank you and he started kissing me, nicely of course, like a good old dear loving dad, saying what a good girl I was. And then he grabbed me."

"What did you do?"

"I kneed him in the nuts. Then I stayed out of the house until my mother came home."

"Did you tell her?" Trace asked.

"Of course I did. Hey, Dick Tracy, this was just one time. That man has found more reasons to pat me on the ass and brush against my boobs than a porcupine's got quills. But this time I told her."

"And what'd she do?"

"Nothing. She never does anything. She lets him beat her, for Christ's sake. He comes home with lipstick on his shirt and fingernail marks on his back, and he goes off without ever telling her anything, and she never says a word. Yeah, I told her, but she didn't do anything and I didn't expect that she would."

"So what'd you do?"

"I packed a bag and moved up here. It was a little early because the school wasn't open, but I got lucky. Found a job at the gym downstairs and that's where I met Julio. So I make a few bucks, add it to what my mother sends me, and pay my debts to higher education. You understand why I don't like my stepfather?"

"I'm getting the idea," Trace said. "You said he comes home with lipstick and scratches. He's a skirt-chaser?"

"The worst," she said.

"Is that hearsay? Or do you know? Do you know any names?"

She shrugged. "I don't know any names, but I can recognize a duck when I see a duck."

"You ever hear of a woman named Mandy in connection with Collins?"

"No, but if there is one, I hope she gives him the clap."

"You say you're paying your own tuition, you and your mother. Why doesn't Collins help?"

"I heard him tell my mother one night that I'm not his real daughter, so why should he pay for her mistakes? Imagine, as rich as that bastard is."

"Nice guy," Trace said.

"They don't make them like that anymore. That's for sure."

"What are you studying?" Trace asked.

"Business. Julio and I are going to open our own place when I graduate."

"With what? It takes money to open a gym."

She smiled icily. "Julio'll be Mister Universe by then," she said.

"Or maybe Collins will die and leave you and your mother a lot of money in life insurance."

The cold smile never left the young woman's face. "That would be nice too," she said. "Especially the part about him dying. Too bad he doesn't like my mother or me well enough to take out a policy."

"This time you're wrong," Trace said. "He already has."

A moment later, Chico, looking none the worse for wear, came from the other room, and she and Trace walked toward the door.

Before leaving, Trace asked Tammy, "You ever hear Collins mention going to a farm somewhere?"

She shook her head and rose from the couch. She could have been truly lovely, Trace realized, if there weren't a hard bitter set to her mouth and her eyes.

"He's hardly the farming type," she said.

"Thanks a lot," Trace said.

"Thank the Nip. She's the one who saved you from Julio," Tammy said.

"Now you can save the world from him," Trace said.

"How's that?"

"See if you can get him into the tub."

17

Only ten minutes into the drive and Chico already looked hungry. Trace tried to take her mind off food. "So what were you doing with that musclebound dwarf so long back there?" It was the first time he'd spoken to her since leaving Tammy Collins' apartment.

"Exercising," Chico said blandly.

"I'll bet. The old pelvic thrust, huh?"

"You have not only a dirty mind but a suspicious one. I'd never fool around with someone who smelled like that."

"No?"

"Not with you in the next room," Chico said.

"Very funny," Trace said.

"I had him show me their bedroom too," she said.

"I'm sure you're not going to leave out one gory detail either, are you?" Trace said.

"I wanted to see if the little bitch had Evening in Byzantium, Trace. I was on the job, as usual."

"Did she?"

Chico's mouth twisted in a grimace of disgust. "No. She had some kind of red-dot special toilet water from the local supermarket. Two bucks the gallon. I found Julio very attractive, though."

"Talk on," Trace said. "Just wait till my rendezvous with Mandy."

"If she uses the same deodorant Julio does, be my guest. I poured Tammy's toilet water over his head before I left."

"Did you really?"

"It was do or die," she said. "And I'm too young to die."

"Well, you brought all those attentions on yourself," Trace said. "Don't forget that, because I won't."

"Don't I know that," she said.

"I have to admit it. I felt some little twinge of conscience about seeing a beautiful call girl. But that was before you and Julio. Now I go with a clear mind and lance a-tilt."

Trace turned off the main highway and Chico said, "Where are you going? You're not trying to spirit me off to some secluded spot to practice lance-tilting for Mandy, are you?"

"You wish," Trace said. "No, I think Mandy will handle the lance very well on her own. We're going to stop by Collins' farm."

"What for?"

"It's not too far out of the way. We might have left some traces of our visit the last time. I just want to make sure that everything's clean."

Chico shook her head. "This is just the way criminals behave, going back to the scene of the crime. Everybody knows you shouldn't do that. It's how people get caught."

"Good," Trace said. "Maybe we'll catch someone."

Though the house was exactly as they had left it, Trace and Chico walked through it again with Chico swiping with a damp cloth at anything she might have missed the last time.

Back outside, they walked toward the barn and Chico said, "That's strange."

"What is?"

"The barn door's unlocked," she said, pointing to the bolt. "We locked it when we left. I remember checking it."

Trace backed Chico away, then took a deep breath, opened the door, and went inside.

After checking that nothing in the barn had been disturbed, Trace kicked aside some of the grass that covered the body. Collins' body was lying in the same position it had been, looking a little worse for wear.

Then he saw something glitter through a thin layer of grass cuttings. Trying to keep

from retching, he pried open Collins' clenched
fingers. Resting on the crawling palm was a
woman's necklace, a diamond butterfly on a
gold chain.

Trace wiped it off with some grass and carried it outside, where he gulped fresh lungfuls
of air.

"He was holding this," he told Chico, ex-
tending the necklace.

"How'd we miss it before?" she said.

"I don't know. It was hard to see. Maybe
the light just hit it the right way today," he
said.

She shook her head. "Or else it wasn't there
before," she said.

"It was probably there. Nothing else was
touched."

"Except the front door," she said. "We locked
it but now it was unlocked. And I looked at
that body, Trace. I checked his wallet, for
Pete's sake. I would have seen a necklace if he
was holding it."

"Why do you try to make everything more
complicated?" Trace asked. "Don't I have
enough problems? Why would anyone plant a
diamond necklace on a corpse?"

"Obviously to create a false trail," Chico
said smugly.

"You'd better stick to seducing fireplug
dwarfs," Trace said. He pocketed the necklace.

"You're not going to keep that thing, are
you?"

"Not keep keep," he said, "just borrow."

"You're real bad, Trace. First you don't call the cops when you should. And now you're removing evidence from the scene of a crime. You'll go up the river for twenty years. Fifty, when I turn state's evidence and rat on you."

"Don't worry. I'm going to turn the necklace over to the cops. In time."

"How much time?" she asked.

"Enough time to find out how it got there if it wasn't there the last time."

"I know how it got there. Whoever murdered Collins put it there so some crazy would pick it up and take the blame from the cops."

"I know it's difficult for women sometimes, but please try to be logical," Trace said smugly. "As I am. I intend to confront Mandy the Hooker with this necklace and force the truth out of her."

"Hold her down, Trace. You always do better with women when you hold them down."

"Don't be jealous. It ill-becomes you," Trace said.

"Get crabs and die," Chico said.

From the hotel he called Mandy's phone number again. This time, he did not pretend to be Thomas Collins but gave her his real name. Mandy said she'd love to meet him for cocktails in an hour and gave him an address near Russian Hill.

He was clipping his frog microphone to his tie when Chico walked into the room.

"How's your mother?" he asked.

"She's fine. Fully recovered. You're going to see Mandy?"

"All in the line of duty. I promise you I won't enjoy a minute of it." He took a Polaroid photograph of the butterfly-shaped necklace and put it in his pocket.

"You never look this good for me," Chico said.

"I always look this way. Exactly this good."

"The hell you do. All I ever see you in is rippedy jeans and hair grease."

"Don't knock the jeans. It took years to get them to look like that."

"Maybe I should go with you," Chico said.

"I don't think so."

"She'll be able to snow you with her sex appeal," Chico said. "You'll need a cooler head around than either of yours."

"Couldn't do it, Chico. This might be a dangerous mission."

"Right," Chico said. "I can tell by your combat-ready silk handkerchief."

"Don't be that way. If it makes you feel any better, I want you to know I'll be thinking of your pinched little food-stuffed face during every ecstatic moment." He kissed her on both cheeks and saluted. "We who are about to disrobe salute you."

"Keep it zipped, Trace," she warned.

"I will."

"If you don't, I'll know."

"How will you know?" he asked.

"I always know."

Trace blew her a kiss and left. She was right: she always knew.

18

The name on the doorbell said M. REESE. Trace was admitted to the apartment by a maid, white, middle-aged, sow-faced, wearing a black nylon uniform and practical white ripple-soled shoes.

He was invited to make himself confortable for a few minutes in a living room whose opulence made the Araby Casino high-rollers' room look like a Social Security office. Through mirrors, the living room seemed to stretch for blocks, showing off a lot of modern furniture and several huge arrangements of exotic flowers. Trace touched one. The flowers were dried, and he thought that was a good symbol for a high-priced hooker: exotic and dried.

Mandy Reese swept into the room like Loretta Young staging a comeback. She wore a Grecian-style gown gathered over one shoulder with a clasp of diamonds and pearls. She was a stunner, attractive enough for magazine covers, with large gray eyes and full lips and the kind of patrician nose that Trace decided had never smelled sauerkraut.

Trace started to speak, but she raised a finger to her lips to shush him while she went to the bar and poured both of them drinks in cut-crystal glasses. She hit a button and soft romantic music enveloped them from hidden speakers all over the room.

When she handed him the glass, Trace said, "Thank you. Nice place."

He sipped the drink. It was Scotch, but good Scotch and therefore bearable.

"Thank you," she said. "It's home, with all the comforts. Such as beds, for instance. Do you know it costs me two hundred dollars an hour to rent this place? Then there are extras, like bathtubs and rooms for body rubs and saunas. Living here for an hour, if I turn on all the extras, costs me about three hundred dollars."

She gave Trace a dazzling smile. Her voice was soft and Trace thought maybe New England. He figured he was probably mistaken: if she had really been from New England, she would already have had his money in her garter belt or wherever she kept it.

Trace took out his wallet and placed three one-hundred-dollar bills on a mirror-topped coffee table.

"Is this for me?" she said. Her eyes smiled right along with her mouth.

"Yes," Trace said.

"A gift for me?" she repeated.

Trace was beginning to wonder why he had bothered to turn on his tape recorder. Mandy Reese was obviously taping this conversation herself, just to prove that she had not solicited anyone for purposes of prostitution. Just in case the matter ever reared its ugly head.

"Yes, a gift for you," Trace said. "Given willingly and with no hint or promise of future considerations. Out of the goodness of my heart, which is monumental both in size and in its capacity for compassion."

Mandy Reese laughed. She laughed easily, a woman very confident of herself. She scooped up the three bills, put them in a little stone vase atop the tiled fireplace, then turned and said, "It's always good to get all that out of the way. Now what kind of partying do you want to do?"

"Sit and let's enjoy this drink," Trace said. He waved an idle hand around the apartment. "You seem to make a pretty good living in a town with San Francisco's reputation. Just imagine how you'd do in the Klondike."

"Give me those long winter nights every time," she said lightly. "But you're right. Forty percent of the men in this town are gay. The other sixty percent are broke. But then there's some married ones who are straight and have money. Those are my kind of friends," she said.

"Police?" Trace asked. "Aren't you pretty visible?"

"They wouldn't bother me. I mean, this is a

town where they've got he-ing and he-ing going on right on Main Street at High Noon. You think there they're going to bother me for promoting a little old-fashioned he-ing and she-ing?" She sat on the sofa next to Trace and crossed her legs, exposing a creamy-white thigh.

"Speaking of he-ing and she-ing, what are you up for?" she asked silkily.

"Basically, I'd like to talk."

"Sure. For sixty minutes, we can talk about anything from Petrarchan sonnets to quarks. I'm yours, Devlin. Talk away."

"Call me Trace," he said.

She put her right hand gently on his left thigh. "Whatever you want, Trace. Whatever."

"I was hoping you'd feel that way. Basically I wanted to talk about insurance." He looked at her and watched her face change from candlelight to molten steel.

"If you want to talk about insurance, perhaps you should talk to my partners," she said. She started to rise from the couch, but Trace grabbed her wrist.

"Not that kind of insurance. Not shakedown stuff. Mandy, I work for an insurance company."

She softened and sat back down. Then she laughed. "You didn't invest that three hundred dollars to try to get me to buy a policy, did you? If you did, you've got to be the dumbest insurance man in the world."

"No. I'm an investigator with an insurance

company and I'm looking into a case, and I thought you might be able to give me some information."

"What kind of information?"

"Nothing heavy and all confidential," Trace said.

She was silent as she took three sips from her drink. Then she relaxed back against the couch and said, "I don't trust it, but why don't you give it a try?"

"Fair enough," Trace said. "Does the name Thomas Collins mean anything to you?"

"A drink that gives you a toothache," she said.

"No, a man," Trace said.

"No."

"Never heard the name before?" he asked.

"Never."

"Mandy, that's not quite accurate. I called you two days ago using that name."

"Trace, truth. If you asked me if I know John Smith, I'd say no and I get fifty calls a day using that name. If you called me saying Tom Collins, I wouldn't remember it for two minutes."

"Okay," Trace said. "That's logical and I apologize. Think hard now, though. Thomas Collins. Forty-ish, needle-nosed, thin white hair fluffed around his ears, real-estate man."

"Maybe," she said. "But I don't remember everybody who comes here real well. What about him?"

"He's dead."

"Does this concern me?" she asked.

"He had your phone number on him," Trace said.

"Balls," she said. She stood up and paced. "Okay, I remember him. But you were talking about cuff links on the telephone. I don't know anything about any cuff links."

"Then you do remember my call."

"When I think I might be getting involved in something," she said, "my memory improves remarkably. I knew you weren't him 'cause he had a high squeaky voice."

"You're not getting involved, Mandy. The police don't even know about this, and as far as I'm concerned, they're not going to."

"What about the cuff links?" she asked.

"He got a note in the mail from someone named Mandy. There was a cuff link with it."

"Wrong girl," she said. "I don't return presents. Even if it is only one cuff link."

"How about a diamond necklace?" Trace said. He searched her face for a reaction, but there was none.

"If I wouldn't return a single cuff link I certainly wouldn't give back a diamond necklace. But the fact is I don't have one."

He handed her the Polaroid of the butterfly necklace.

"Ever see that before?"

"Please," she said, handing it back. "That's too tacky for Peoria. But it's something that he would buy."

"How's that?"

"It looks like it came out of a gumball machine. That was Collins' style."

"Tell me about him," Trace said. "Did he come here often?"

"The last few years, every so often, but he's no regular. Collins was sort of a quarterly client."

"When was the last time?"

"A couple of months ago, the early part of the summer, I guess. He invited me to go to Las Vegas and gamble with him. As if I'd be caught dead outside this apartment with that pig."

"He was no special favorite of yours, I take it," Trace said.

She laughed without humor. "He had no class, absolutely none. He'd come in here waving cash around like it gave him the biggest dong in California and talking about all the girls he'd been with."

"Anyone special?"

"Special how?"

Trace sipped his drink. "I don't know. Love relationships, maybe."

Mandy rocked with laughter and sat down again next to Trace. "Hell, no. Showgirls, stuff like that. He claimed to be a high-roller at the Fontana in Vegas. I suppose the casino fixed him up. I can't imagine anybody would trick with him unless somebody was paying for it."

"He was bad?" Trace asked.

"In the sack? Strictly zero. He wouldn't be

able to get it up and then he'd get mad about it and say it was because he was with sixteen different women in the last two days."

"Isn't that annoying to you?" Trace asked.

Her features softened and she shook her head. "All in a day's entertaining." She stroked his thigh. "I know how to handle things like that. Any more questions?"

"He ever tell you that he had a farm?"

"No. Any more questions?"

"Why do you advertise in sleazy papers?" Trace asked.

"I haven't advertised in a year. As far as my finances are concerned, you might say I'm on my feet. Any more questions?"

"Would Collins have to keep a copy of your ad around for any reason?"

She shook her head. "He always carried this little address book in his wallet. His little book of lust, he called it. He said my number was in there. Anyway, I'm in the phone book too. Any more questions?"

"A couple. He ever talk about anybody?"

"Like what? Like who?"

"Like how he got along with people," Trace said. "Like his business, his family. Try the wife."

"You mean besides that his wife didn't understand him," Mandy said with a laugh.

"Maybe something a little more original," Trace said.

"Here. Let me fix up that drink," she said.

Mandy took Trace's glass from his hand and walked to the bar. She was very nice to look at from behind and Trace didn't mind the view but he thought she was taking an awfully long time to pour scotch and ice into a glass.

She was going to drug him. Trace knew it. She had poured some particularly noxious chemical into his drink and she was going to stir it until the very last granule dissolved. Then she was going to make him drink it and then she'd laugh while he struggled to stay awake before finally lapsing into unconsciousness on the couch.

And then . . .

And then what?

She surely wasn't going to rob him. She already had his three hundred dollars and Trace knew he didn't give the impression of somebody who was carrying five million bucks around inside the toe of his shoe.

Murder him? Not unless she had killed Collins. Had Trace pried too far and too deep? Was this it for him? Would they harpoon his body out of San Francisco Bay in three days?

Maybe she was a white slaver? Maybe Trace was going to be drugged and stuck in the hold of a sheep ship then sent to Saudi Arabia where he'd have to spend the rest of his life making love to fat Arabian princesses. A concubine in a country without a decent drink in it.

Maybe he should run. Race for the door now and get out of there while he still could.

What would a real detective do?

He thought about it and decided a real detective would have another drink. And a ploy.

"That's nice perfume you're wearing," he said cleverly. "Is that Evening in Byzantium?"

"I'm not wearing perfume," she said, her back still turned.

"I would have sworn it was Evening in Byzantium," Trace said sourly. What was it Chico had said? "Patachouli, cinnamon, lemon grass, a hint of something else."

"What are you, a perfume expert?" she asked over her shoulder.

"I know something about it," Trace said modestly.

"Well, I hate Evening in Byzantium. There's a metallic high note there I can't stand."

What was this, Trace wondered. Everybody in the world knew everything about perfume except him. The only two smells he could distinguish from each other were Drano fumes and dog breath. Three. He could also tell the smell of dead bodies, corpses as ripe as his own would soon be if Mandy wasn't stopped from stirring that poison into his drink.

Mandy suddenly turned from the bar, walked forward, stuck the glass into his hand, and said, "All right," like a woman who had just made a decision. "Wait here a moment," she said.

When she went out the door at the end of the room, Trace held the drink up to the light. There. There was something in it. Probably a fleck of poison. It looked like a brine shrimp. A big fleck of poison. What kind of fool did she think he was?

He walked to the bar and poured the drink down the sink. Then he rinsed the glass quickly, put fresh ice cubes and Scotch into it, and hurried back to his seat on the sofa. He was sipping the drink when Mandy returned.

She sat next to him on the couch.

"You were asking?" she said.

Trace nodded. "What Collins might have said about business or family."

"Okay," she said.

"Good drink, by the way," he said and watched her eyes for a suspicious reaction.

"Same as the last. It's hard to mess up Scotch and ice cubes," she said.

"There's a special metallic high note," he said.

"That's my ice-cube maker. I don't think the maid washed all the soap out of the trays. I keep seeing these little flecks in the drinks. I had to mix three drinks for you before I got a clean one."

"Oh," Trace said. So much for murder and white slaving.

"Anyway, Collins never talked about his business except to say that he was a big rich real estate developer. He had lots of money all the time but that was just his way of trying to impress me."

"Staying in character," Trace said and Mandy nodded and sipped some of her drink.

"But he did talk about the family once in a while," she said.

"Yes?"

"He said his wife, that's Judith, was dull and uninteresting."

"I guess you've heard that one before," Trace said.

"He said that she was a beauty when he married her but then she let herself go. She didn't use makeup any more; she was going to be an artist and she was making herself look artsy-fartsy with no makeup and letting her hair grow every which way and he didn't even want to sleep with her anymore."

"Did he say they ever fought about it?"

"He said they never fought about anything, that she was afraid to fight with him. She was stubborn, though, in her wimpy way. She wouldn't do what he said, not even pluck her eyebrows. And then there was a Tammy. That's his daughter."

"Stepdaughter," Trace said.

"He hated her," Mandy said.

"How's that?"

"He said she was a little tramp who was putting out for everybody. He said that he thought she went through his wallet all the time stealing money."

"What kind of kid would she be if she didn't try to steal money from her parents?" Trace asked. "Especially a tight-fisted one like him."

"There was more to it than that," Mandy said, as she put down her drink and placed her hand easily on Trace's right thigh.

"How so?" Trace asked.

"He said she was a . . . well, the precise phrase was sleazy little bitch. He said that whenever the mother was out, little Tammy would lounge around the house with nothing on and try to put the make on him."

"Did she ever get lucky, I wonder?" Trace said.

"Once," Mandy said. "He said they spent an afternoon once playing around a little bit and then she tried to shake him down. She wanted him to lend her enough money to start a business and if he didn't, she was going to tell her mother that he molested her."

"He didn't buy it?"

"No. And according to him, he told her that if she really needed money, she should go out and peddle it on the street."

"Nice people," Trace said. "Anything else?"

"That's all I had," Mandy said. She made light circles on Trace's thigh with the palm of her hand.

"You mind my asking . . ." Trace said.

Mandy stirred her drink with her finger. "No. You're going to ask how'd I suddenly remember all this stuff. I could diddle you around but I'm going to tell you the truth—I keep notes on my regulars. It's better for business to know what worries them and be able to drop names into the conversation. They start thinking of you as a friend, someone they can talk to and that keeps them coming back. When I left the room, I went and looked in my notes. That's what I had."

"You told me all of it?" Trace said.

"Hey. In for a penny, in for a pound. If I were going to tell you anything at all—and I didn't have to—why shouldn't I tell you everything?"

"That makes sense," Trace conceded.

She was still rubbing his leg and Trace wished that she would stop. He didn't wish it a lot; it was just a little wish.

She leaned over and kissed his ear wetly. "You've still got twenty minutes," she said softly. "Want to use it?"

"Yes. I mean no." He wished he'd never met Chico Mangini and her telepathic guilt waves.

"It's your loss," she said.

"I'm sure it is," Trace said. He drained the last of his Scotch.

"You're one of the forty percent, aren't you?" she asked as accusingly.

"Forty percent?"

"The forty percent gays in this town," she said.

"If only," Trace said. "If only."

She looked at him and nodded her head. "Okay. For you, I'll issue a raincheck. What happens with Collins?"

"First he was missing and now he's dead. I just want to see if there was anything flukey about it before my insurance company pays off."

"I'm sorry I couldn't help much," Mandy said, "Collins was a regular but not like clockwork. And I didn't write any note about cuff links. I'm not going to be involved, am I?"

"Not if I have anything to do with it," Trace said.

"Thank you," she said. "I may wind up owing you; I hope you come back to collect."

Trace reached inside his jacket pocket and switched off the tape recorder, then said: "I just may take you up on that."

"You won't be sorry," Mandy Reese said.

The maid showed him out. When the apartment door had closed behind him, Trace turned on the tape recorder and then spoke toward the microphone on his necktie.

"Never," he said. "Never could I entertain such a thought. Not I, who has the most wonderful woman in the world waiting for me back at my room. I am offended, madam, by such a suggestion and I now take my leave of you. Good-bye forever."

He clicked the recorder off and entered the elevator, smiling smugly. Let Chico listen in on this tape. It'd be a lesson to her—Chico's own custom-made seminar on the last honorable man in an ever-changing world.

Wonderful.

19

Trace was relieved to see the pink message note hanging out of the mailbox for his room. Rather than face Chico and her inevitable accusations, Trace was willing to call anyone— including Judith Collins.

"I've notified the police of my husband's absence," Mrs. Collins said.

"Good. What did they say?"

"Well, I talked to them only this morning, but they didn't seem too hopeful. It seems a lot of men disappear every year. Honestly, Mr. Tracy, I don't think they're going to be much help. I'd appreciate it if you'd stay on the case. Of course, I'm prepared to pay you whatever your fee is."

Trace ran through his priorities. First there was the convention, where he was doomed to endless samurai movies and having Mr. Nishimoto harass him about Bataan. Missing that would be no great loss. And if he socked Mrs. Collins for a fee and then collected a fee from

178

Garrison Fidelity too, this case would be a double-dip. Not bad for a school-of-hard-knocks graduate.

And then there was the indisputable fact that Thomas Collins had been murdered and somebody out there was getting away with it. That offended his sense of neatness and order.

Trace sighed. Screw the fee. Find that baseball-bat-swinging bastard.

"Are you there, Mr. Tracy?"

"Yes. I'll keep looking for your husband," Trace said. "Don't worry about the fee."

"You're very kind. Much too kind."

"Tell that to the IRS when I ask them to send me donations," he said.

"Have you learned anything?" she asked hopefully.

Trace had already decided not to tell her that her husband was as dead as a doornail until he could announce with a flourish, "And here's the son of a bitch who killed him." Presenting the mad batter might ease her pain a little whereas delivering just a corpse might send her over the edge. Trace didn't want to be talking to a hysterical woman by phone, not when another hysterical woman was undoubtedly up in his room waiting for him to report in.

Trace said blandly, "I've run across a few things. Did your husband ever mention the Fontana Hotel in Las Vegas to you?"

She thought a moment. "No, I don't think so," she said. "Is it a casino thing?"

"Yes. There's a casino."

"Well, no, Thomas never mentioned any such place. We're not gamblers, Mr. Tracy."

"Do you know if your husband has a small black address book?" He was finding it difficult to keep talking about Collins in the present tense as if he were not moldering away in a barn.

"No. I never saw any address book. There's the Rolodex in his office. Do you need a phone number? I could look it up."

"No, thanks. Just one more thing. Did you ever see a butterfly necklace?"

"Er, I don't think so. What's it made of?"

"Oh, glass. Rhinestones maybe. I thought Thomas might have given it to you or your daughter."

"It doesn't ring a bell. Thomas doesn't believe in spending money on frivolous things like jewelery."

"No. That makes sense," Trace said. He promised to get back to her as soon as anything turned up, then hung up the lobby phone. It was obvious that Mrs. Collins knew less about her husband than just about anyone else who'd ever been associated with the man.

And now to face Chico.

Well, what did she want from him anyway? It was only his oversized sense of honor that had kept him from shagging Mandy Reese right on her rented couch. It certainly wasn't all the sexual satisfaction he'd been getting with Chico, who, because her mother was sleeping in the room next door, had put Trace on hold. A man had needs, didn't she know that?

Yes, he told himself, she knew that. She also knew that one of a man's biggest needs was to stay alive, so all in all he was glad that he'd said no to Mandy and that he had a tape recording to prove it.

Trace paused outside his room door, rehearsing the scene that was sure to come. Chico would be sitting at the table, reading a book. She would put down the book, drum her pointy little fingers on the table, and accuse him of philandering.

He would be hurt. She would be disbelieving.

And then he would play the tape recording for her and she would crumble to guilty powder in front of him.

He thought about it again. It sounded pretty good. It ought to play.

He found his key and unlocked the door. Chico was not at the table. Instead, she lay on the bed, a vision from an Art Deco print. Her eyes were painted like a China doll's and her lips were red as candy apples. She was wearing a short red silk robe that showed off her long smooth legs, all the way down to some kind of feathered slippers on her feet.

She said nothing as he came into the room, only smiled at him as if she'd been waiting for him all her life.

"Before you start on me," he said, "I didn't do anything."

"I know." She pulled him close to her and as their lips met, the silk gown fell away.

"What about your mother?"

"She's at the movies," Chico said.

"It may end soon," Trace said.

"A triple feature. Sixteen, seventeen, and eighteen Samurai."

"Hooray for Horrywood," Trace said.

Afterward, they lay in bed, smoking cigarettes. Chico smoked only after making love and Trace believed the same was true of millions of women. If he were a chemist, he'd create a birth-control ingredient that could be mixed with tobacco. Make love, smoke a cigarette, and don't worry about a thing. And the upshot was that only totally confirmed nonsmokers would have unwanted children. That sociological side effect seemed fair too. Unwanted children for holier-than-thou adults. He decided that to mention it now would ruin the moment but he promised himself to look into it. This idea was a winner. Right up there with the Q-Tip and the Band-Aid.

Chico said, "What are you thinking about?"

"Oh, one man's place in the cosmos, the role of each of us in the big scheme of things."

"I thought you'd be thinking about Thomas Collins," she said. "Are you going to hand it over to the cops?"

"Look at it this way," Trace said. "If I tell the cops what I know now, my ass is in a sling for not reporting it all right away. But if I tell them all of it *and* who killed him, then I'm off the hook. I may even get a medal."

"Or at least escape a jail sentence," she said. "So you're sticking with the case."

"Why not? I hate samurai movies. By the way, I'd like you to do something for me."

"Something else?" Chico said. "I thought I'd just brought out the whole arsenal."

"Smut mind," Trace said. "For your information, there are some of us who are not always obsessed with sex. Now back to the Collins case. Who do we know at the Fontana?"

"I know Anselmo real well."

"Who's he?" Trace asked.

"He's floor boss most nights. He's a good guy. You met him once."

"Can you talk to him?"

"Yup."

"Find out if he knows anything about Collins. I've heard he was a high-roller at the Fontana. See if we can get anything on how much he spent, how often he was there, things like that. Women, too, if any."

"Sure," Chico said. She reached for the telephone, but Trace put his hand on hers.

"I'm still thinking," he said. He rolled out of bed and said, "I'm going to do my log." From the dresser drawer, he got the butterfly necklace.

"Why don't you go downstairs and ask them if this is real?"

"It's real," Chico said.

"Can you smell diamonds too? I can understand Evening in Byzantium, but diamonds too?"

"Diamonds too. Sweetest smell in the world next to you," she said.

20

Trace's Log: Tape Number Two, six-thirty P.M. Wednesday, two more tapes in the master file, Devlin Tracy in the matter of Thomas Collins.

To know him was to hate him, I guess. It looks like Collins handed everyone he met a calling card and a very good reason to use his head for batting practice. Like Tammy, the stepdaughter. She says attempted rape. But what that snotty little bitch calls attempted rape Collins said was attempted seduction and blackmail. Make that actual seduction, not attempted. Who'd believe either one of them? They're not exactly a family out of "Father Knows Best."

I don't know if it took a lot of power to bash in Collins' head that way, but if it did that musclebound cretin Tammy's shacked up with has got the stuff. And a motive since the two of them want to open a gym of their own. Them that sweat together, get together, I guess.

Do they also blackmail together? Or go halfies on a murder/insurance policy package?

I don't know. Maybe it's just that I don't like the boyfriend who was going to do a clean and jerk on me until Chico started feeling him up.

Clean and jerk. At least, he's got the jerk part down right.

And then we've got Mandy Reese whom (Chico, if you're listening, and I have tape recordings to back me up) I not only did not score with but I spurned. You hear me? *Spurned.*

I will not forget to put in my expenses to Groucho Marks on this one. At three hundred dollars an hour, talking to Mandy is a very expensive proposition. Make it four hundred, counting taxi fare and the wear and tear on my endocrine system.

Anyway, Mandy didn't think any more of Collins than Tammy did, and she got paid for her enthusiasm.

Mandy's the one who told me about Collins' run-in with the stepdaughter. Mandy keeps notes. God help us. The next thing you know the hookers of the world will invest in Apple Computers and each and every one of us will be catalogued in a whore's memory disc somewhere. Please, whoever is listening to this, no jokes about hard and floppy. This has not been the kind of day for levity.

Anyway, from what Mandy says, Collins was a big mouth who flashed cash and waved a black book around with all his women's names in it. What a crock, though. As the saying goes, 'If you're smart, why aren't you rich?' Okay, Collins. If you're irresistible, why are you paying for it?

So a couple of months ago, Collins invited Mandy to go to Vegas. We'll see if he spent much time there. I'm sure the guy was making a buck in real estate, and since he spent all of about two cents on the dollar on his wife and home, he dropped a bundle someplace. If you go to Vegas often enough, you're going to come up empty, so maybe Mabley was right. Maybe there was a little fast-and-loose going on with real-estate-agency money.

And Mandy nixed the cuff link. So who prints a note, signs it Mandy, and sends Collins' cuff link back to his post-office box? That means something, but I'll be damned if I know what.

There's no shortage of mysteries here, that's for sure. The butterfly necklace. Chico's probably right: that wasn't in Collins' hand when we saw him the first time. So how'd it get there now? I mean, somebody finds a body, sticks a piece of jewelry in the hand as a farewell gift, and then beats it without calling the cops? That really doesn't scan.

I have to figure something out here pretty soon. Mrs. Collins called the cops and somebody's probably going to find him pretty soon. Certainly before he turns to farina. Thank God for Chico. If there's an answer in here, she'll come up with it. If you're listening to this,

Chico, I want you to know I mean it. I may razz you a lot because you're little and yellow, and eat much too much. But you are also the smartest woman I've ever met in my life. Except for Mrs. Grunewald, who ran the grocery store when I was growing up.

Trace signing off for now. Today's expenses, travel, hookers, much food for Chico, telephone calls, many things, call it an even thousand. The Collins story may not be adding up but the charges are.

21

As Trace put the tape recorder away into the top dresser drawer, Chico popped back into the room.

"Finished recording your memoirs, Casanova? My Day with Mandy, the Hooker?"

"If I could handle Mandy *and* you in one day, I'd send my parts off to be bronzed."

Chico tossed the necklace onto the bed. "The diamonds are real. The jeweler downstairs verified it. He said they're not high quality, but they're real."

"Good work," Trace said.

"We're having dinner with my mother in twenty minutes," Chico said as she sat down and crisply opened a small notebook.

"You need a notebook now to keep track of our dinner dates?" he asked.

"The notebook's for detective work, stupid. Doesn't it look official? Just be quiet and listen. Collins used to go to the Fontana ten or twelve times a year."

"By himself?"

"Usually. Or with a boom-boom girl. Never his wife."

"High-roller?" Trace asked.

"A lowlife. Credit line for two or three thousand. He'd try to nickel and dime the casino with small bets, then he'd complain because everything wasn't complimentary. He busted Anselmo's chops once because the casino wouldn't pick up his airfare."

"Then he sounds like a lot of other people," Trace said. "Spending a little and getting the most they can for it."

"Except for the last time he was there. That was . . ." She consulted her notebook.

"Oh, will you stop it with that notebook?" Trace said. "The next thing I know you'll buy a freaking magnifying glass."

"It's on the way up. I charged it to your room. He was there about two weeks ago, let's see, September twenty-first weekend. Anselmo says Collins dropped twenty-five thousand at the blackjack tables in three days. The hotel comped him and it was a good thing they did because he blew his last nickel at the tables. Wipeout City. He even asked the girl he was with to hand over her necklace so he could hock it."

Trace turned around from the dresser where he had been stacking his tapes. "What did the necklace look like?"

"Guess."

"Then . . ."

"I'm way ahead of you. See, aren't you glad I got this notebook to write everything down? Collins bought the necklace at the jewelry store in the Fontana on the first night he was there. At that point, he was small winner. Anselmo couldn't give me a description of the woman Collins was with, but he said she was sitting alongside him, playing, so he's got videotape with them on it from the eye-in-the-sky cameras. He's going to get us a print."

Trace raised his eyebrows and sat alongside Chico on the bed.

"You're tough. I've got to hand it to you."

"Don't thank me. My work carries a price."

Trace sighed. "My body again, I suppose," he said. "Well, go ahead. I'll make the sacrifice."

"I'll give you my bill later," she said. "I don't think you'll get off that easily."

She opened the door between the two rooms and said, "Get dressed for dinner."

Trace had a drink, got dressed, then belted down another one.

He was drinking too much again. As much as he bitched at Chico for making him stick to wine, she was his only hope: Trace was no longer able to control his vodka intake. Not that he had ever done much controlling in the past, but his younger body was better able to withstand the assaults of the booze.

He had always bragged of never having had a hangover but now, every morning after, his head felt stuffed with cotton balls and his mouth was an excrescence. He wasn't as sharp as he used to be on the job. He missed things. And his temper, always short to begin with, now hovered on the edge of start-swinging fury.

"Time to get your crap together, Trace," he mumbled to himself in the growing darkness of the hotel room. Then he thought of having dinner again with Mr. Nishimoto, and he poured the last of the vodka into his glass. He'd get himself together tomorrow.

He called Walter Marks at home.

"It's Trace."

"So soon? I left an urgent message only two days ago that you should call me."

"I've been busy. What did you want?"

"I talked to Mike Mabley. He told me that you're working on the Collins matter," Marks said.

"That's right," Trace said.

"Why did you tell him my name was Groucho?" Marks demanded.

"Did I do that?"

"You did."

"Well, I was joking. Your friends don't have much in the way of a sense of humor. Which is strange, considering that they're your friends."

"Have you found out anything?" Marks asked.

"Just that this is a rotten way to waste a vacation and that you're going to pay for it," Trace said.

"Well, Mabley told me that you were being helpful and I wanted to thank you."

Trace sipped his drink before answering. "Well, Groucho, he's been helpful too," he said earnestly.

"Oh? How's that?"

Trace tried to think of some way Mabley had been helpful. Finally, he said, "He gave me a lift in his car when it was raining."

"He probably just wanted you to see it," Marks said. "It's his pride and joy—his first Lincoln."

"I'm thrilled for him," Trace said.

"It's useless to try to be friendly with you," Marks said.

"Go sit on a pickle," Trace said.

"You ought to say a prayer every night to Bob Swenson. If he wasn't the president of this company, you'd be down the toilet in a minute."

"That's not nice. Especially after telling Mabley that I was the best man in the business," Trace said.

"I never said any such thing. You must have been drinking too much as usual."

"You didn't tell him that?"

"No. I told him that you were a worthless degenerate, a drunk who spends all his time in gambling dens. That Garrison Fidelity means as much to you as the man in the moon. That you have no respect for money, especially other people's. That Bob Swenson keeps you on the job as a personal favor. That you are usually so booze-soggled that you don't know what case you're working on."

"That all?"

"No. I also told him that you could take every bit of dedication and loyalty in your being and stuff it into a caraway seed."

"Sounds about right to me," Trace said blandly.

"Personally, I wouldn't hire you if you were the last insurance investigator on earth."

"Personally, I'm glad," Trace said.

Marks beat him to hanging up, so Trace was left there with the telephone in his hand. Was he really that bad a person? Was he mean, rotten, and reprehensible, the way Marks said?

Oh, that demon rum. It was responsible for everything.

He dialed a New York number. His father answered.

"Sarge," Trace said. "Am I an alcoholic?"

"Of course you are," Sarge said.

"Wait, wait a minute. Don't be so cavalier. This is a big question. Take some time before answering."

"Okay, son," Sarge said cheerfully. "You tell me when time's up and we'll talk about something else in the meantime."

"All right," Trace said. "How's the private detecting business?" Sarge was a retired New York City policeman who, largely to get out of the house and away from Trace's mother, had just opened a private-detective agency above

Bogie's Restaurant on West Twenty-sixth Street in Manhattan.

"Scratching away, making a few nickels. I may have to move my office, though."

"Don't do anything rash," Trace said. "You could try sweeping it first."

"It's not that. It's the people I have to deal with."

"What do you mean?" Trace asked.

"Downstairs in the restaurant. It's turning into a zoo for whacko private eyes. They got one ex-pug tending bar and he's supposed to be a detective. Christ, I don't know how he got a license, but he makes Jake LaMotta look like Leonardo daVinci."

"So. That's not so bad," Trace said.

"That's not all of it. They got this other p.i. who comes in, and Mary, Mother of God, he sounds like *Pravda*. He sits at the end of the bar, waving his drink in his one good hand and spouting stuff from Karl Marx. The other night, I was listening to him and I said, 'Workers of the World Unite, You Have Nothing to Lose but Your Chains,' and he said, 'Right on, Brother.' I tell you, Trace, the neighborhood's going down the pipes."

"Yeah, but the owner lets you borrow her plants to decorate that mouse nest you call an office, and the rent is right, and you're right up above the best scungille salad in New York, so don't be hasty."

"One more communist private detective and I go," Sarge said.

"Where's Mother?"

"She's out harassing the neighbors," Sarge said.

"How would I find out if a privately owned company was in financial trouble?" Trace asked suddenly.

"Talk to one of their competitors," Sarge answered immediately.

"Thank you. I always know where to come for advice," Trace said. "Now, am I an alcoholic?"

"Son, if you aren't, you're the only male born in our family in six generations who isn't. Is that answer enough?"

"I guess so. I'm thinking about quitting."

"Don't do anything rash," Sarge said.

"It's not rash. I'm going to quit. Thanks for talking to me."

"Anytime," Sarge said.

"Oh. And don't tell Mother I called."

"Why not?"

"She'll expect me to do it again," Trace said.

22

When Trace finally rolled into the hotel's main dining room, Chico and her mother were already in their seats. Mr. Nishimoto's seat, however, was empty.

"I happy to see you, You," Chico's mother said. "This is very important dinner."

"I'm glad I came, Emmie," Trace said. He whispered to Chico, "Where's our friend the masher?"

"Mr. Nishimoto's been on his good behavior since the orange-juice thing," Chico said. "He'll probably be along."

"Good. Listen," Trace said. "I've come to a decision."

"What's that?" Chico asked.

"I . . ." He stopped as someone stepped up to their table. It was Mr. Nishimoto, carrying a dinner napkin in both hands as if it were a king's crown.

Trace saw Emmie eye him cautiously, but Mr. Nishimoto bowed politely to all three of them, then carefully placed the napkin in front of Chico's mother.

"What's he doing?" Trace whispered to Chico. "Why's he giving her a napkin? Is her face dirty?"

"It's a present," Chico said.

"A used restaurant napkin? What a sport."

"He's folded it into the shape of a swan. The ephemeralness of it adds to its beauty."

"The last of the big spenders, obviously," Trace said.

Meanwhile, Emmie Mangini sat stony-faced, not even looking at the napkin.

"I don't think your mother likes this guy," Trace said. "Maybe I ought to show him the door."

"My Japanese is better than yours," Chico said. "I'll do it." She cornered Mr. Nishimoto, like a ferret, Trace thought, and began talking to him in Japanese. Chico had only spoken a few words when Mr. Nishimoto blanched and Emmie crashed her open palm on the tabletop, silencing her daughter as if she had pulled the electric cord on a kitchen utensil.

"That enough, Michiko. I speak English for not to shame Mr. Nishimoto more than you do already. Even so, I have to kill self tomorrow morning for your behavior."

Chico looked stunned. Trace said to her mother, "You told us this guy was a masher, remember?"

"Other day, mash. Today, make swan. Very improvement," Emmie said.

Trace sighed. "You can't argue with logic, I guess."

"Who Rogic?" Mrs. Mangini said. "Is Mr. Nishimoto, remember?"

Trace smiled wanly.

"Mr. Nishimoto is politeness, not fight with womans. Japanese way. My daughter, excuse me, she talk to him like barbarian."

"Must be the company she keeps," Trace said.

"I invite him to be at table again," Emmie said.

Chico said, "Please give him my apologies. Tell him I am heartbroken over my own rudeness."

Mrs. Mangini spoke Japanese to Mr. Nishimoto, who smiled broadly, then took his place at the table. A waiter appeared with a tray of drinks with umbrellas in them.

Each took one and Mr. Nishimoto hoisted his glass toward Trace in salute. "To Bataan," he said.

"Bataan," Trace repeated.

"I'll drink to that," Chico said.

"God breast us every one," Mrs. Mangini said.

Later, Chico said to Trace, "What were you going to tell me before? Something important."

Trace sipped his drink and said, "Forget it. Some other time."

Dinner passed pleasantly. Trace even enjoyed tasting some of the vaguely plasticene foods he was offered. Several umbrella drinks later, he had forgiven everybody and promised to buy cameras for all Emmie's friends at the convention.

He spoke continuously with Mr. Nishimoto. Since "Bataan" was the only word they had in common, it comprised their entire conversation, but it called up a wide range of emotions, from laughing to cheering and finally to open weeping on Mr. Nishimoto's part. In the end, the Japanese man took out a pen and made some marks on his cocktail napkin.

"If he's drawing me a swan, I'm going to hit him," Trace whispered to Chico.

"He writing poem," Emmie said.

"Why? Is he going to kill himself too?"

"Shhhh," Chico cut in. "They're announcing the guest speaker."

Two small men were sharing the microphone at the front of the room, speaking, sometimes separately, sometimes in unison. According to Chico, they were extolling the virtues of a man whose heroism was an inspiration to his country.

"What'd he do?" Trace asked Chico.

"He's a businessman."

"I mean what made him a hero?"

"He got rich," Chico said. "He's the wealthiest Japanese-American in the United States."

"That makes him a hero? Philistines," Trace grumbled.

The two men chattered on for a while longer, then bowed as the audience burst into applause.

"I don't believe it. All this just because some guy got rich?" Trace said to Chico.

"Quiet," Chico said.

Mr. Nishimoto stood up at the table.

"What's with him?" Trace said.

"Mr. Nishimoto is guest of honor," Emmie said delightedly.

"Him? He's the richest Nip in the country?" Trace said.

Chico kicked him under the table.

Mr. Nishimoto walked to the front of the room, slowly, accepting applause. At the podium, he bowed again and then took something out of his pocket. It was the cocktail napkin he had been writing on.

"Hey, that's his poem," Trace said to Chico. Mr. Nishimoto was reading. "What's it about?"

"Bataan," Chico said.

"Pffff," Trace mumbled. "I'd rather watch a samurai movie."

"The poem is about his friend, a great warrior who crushed the enemy under his feet, like beetles, during that great battle."

There was rousing applause. Mr. Nishimoto bowed politely, then continued speaking.

"He says his friend is with us now," Chico translated for Trace. "And the name of this hero of Japan is . . ."

Mr. Nishimoto shouted, "Dev-u-rin Tlacy."

Everyone in the room jumped to their feet and bowed in Trace's direction.

Mrs. Mangini's eyes filled with tears. "I never

know you fight on our side in war," she said proudly.

Trace forced a smile. "I hardly remembered it myself." He whispered to Chico, "The guy's nuts. I never even saw Bataan."

"That doesn't matter," Chico said, a broad smile fixed on her face as if with fiberglass. "Just stand up and bow and we'll get out of here before anyone asks you questions about it."

Trace rose to great applause. Two men brought Mr. Nishimoto a bouquet of roses, which he carried down the aisle and presented to Chico's mother. Then he bowed to Trace, and Trace rose again and bowed back.

"Bataan," Trace said.

"Bataan," Mr. Nishimoto answered with hoarse pride.

Trace leaned over to Chico. "That meant *sayonara*, baby."

"Let's go," she said.

"What about your mother?"

Chico glanced at Emmie, who was staring up at Mr. Nishimoto adoringly.

"I don't think she'll miss us," Chico said. She rose, and with Trace, they backed from the room, bowing all the way.

Outside, Chico started to laugh hysterically.

Trace said, "It's okay for you to laugh, but if the House Committee on Un-American Activities gets hold of this, I'm done for."

"Come on, war hero. I'll buy you a drink," she said.

*   *   *

"So he's the richest guy around," Trace said as they sat in a dark corner of the cocktail lounge. "Who would have believed it?"

"And he's nuts about my mother."

"That's not so surprising," Trace said. "She's beautiful and smart and doesn't talk much funnier than you do, and if I didn't know it'd break your heart, I'd take a run at her myself."

"She wouldn't have you. She also has better taste than I do."

"I wonder what Nishimoto does for a living?" Trace said.

"That Heckle and Jeckle pair of emcees said that he was one of the biggest real-estate developers on the West Coast," Chico said.

"Bingo," Trace said.

"Repeat please."

"I was talking to Sarge. I've got this idea that maybe Collins and Rose are in a little financial bind, and Sarge said the best way to find out is to ask a competitor."

"Your father's a wise man," Chico said.

"He breeds true too," Trace said. "Anyway, I wonder if Mr. Nishimoto could find out if Collins and Rose were on the skids."

"Why not ask him? Here he comes."

Trace turned and saw Nishimoto and Chico's mother enter the cocktail lounge. They moved to a far corner and sat side by side on one of the banquettes. Trace smiled because they looked so formal and ill-at-ease that a chaperone wouldn't have been out of place in the picture.

"Naaah, he'll think I want to buy property on Bataan." Trace said. "He and I have trouble communicating."

"You stay right here. Order me another Perrier," Chico said. "I have to apologize to him anyway."

She left Trace, sat down at her mother's table, and was soon in earnest conversation with Mr. Nishimoto. Finally he nodded and snapped his fingers and the waitress, who had seemed to find no trouble at all in ignoring Trace's frantic attempts to order a drink, instantly appeared at the side of the elderly Japanese man.

He barked a command at her and she set off on a dead run, returning with a telephone that she plugged into a jack in the wall.

Nishimoto spoke on the telephone for five minutes, then hung up and leaned forward and spoke very softly to Chico. She listened, nodding often, then rose, folded her hands in front of her, and bowed slightly to him.

She came back and told Trace, "Your hunch was right. The word is out that Collins and Rose are having deep financial problems."

"Any cause or just the usual business nonsense?" Trace asked.

"That's where your hunch was really right. There are rumors that Collins was dipping into the company treasury."

Trace looked up to see Mr. Nishimoto watching him. When their eyes met, Mr. Nishimoto smiled, raised his glass, and shouted "Baatan" across the room.

Trace smiled back and said to Chico, "Let's get out of here."

23

Trace's Log: Two A.M., Thursday, and Chico has just gone back to her room. Women are nuts. First she wouldn't sleep with me because she's afraid of what her mother will think, and now I think she's getting off because her mother is having a romance with Mr. Nishimoto. But she still wants to be back in her own bed before her mother comes in for the night.

Hah, it'll serve her right if her mother doesn't come home at all. Let her chew on that one for a while.

Anyway, this is Tape Three, and how do you like that one, Groucho, two tapes in the same day? And you think I'm a degenerate who doesn't do any work at all. What a small shallow man you are to so totally misread another's character.

So here are the news headlines since I made that last tape.

One: the diamond necklace is real.

Two: Collins bought it in Las Vegas two

weeks ago just before he dropped twenty-five thousand at the blackjack tables.

Three: my dear old friend, Mr. Nishimoto, checked with some of his Tong warriors and found out that Collins and Rose might be in financial trouble and that Collins might have been dipping into the company treasury.

Four: embezzlement is as good a reason for murder as any.

Five: I don't know why I bother to talk to you, Groucho, now that I have been the guest of honor at a Japanese convention. Just naturally gracious, I guess.

Six: I don't know what I'm going to do with this case. This convention will be packing up its sampans pretty soon and I have this terrible urge to mail the diamond necklace to Mrs. Collins anonymously, dummy up, say I didn't find out anything, and go home and let nature take its course.

Seven: but that means some murderer may just get away with it, and while I suspect Thomas Collins is—was a certifiable shit, somebody ought to go to jail for killing him. This is what comes from being the son of a cop.

Eight: decisions, decisions. One thing you can count on, Walter Marks. I will do the noble thing. Just as I always do.

Nine: this is the hero of Bataan, signing off.

24

Trace was having coffee when his name was paged on the hotel's loudspeaker. He left the coffee and went out to the lobby to find a telephone.

He found both a phone and Chico, who had come out of one of the convention's conference rooms when she heard his name called.

"I wonder who," he said.

"Probably somebody from the Bataan Death March. Wants to blow you away," she said.

"Don't be funny in the morning. I don't like funny in the morning and I don't like pluck. Those are two things I really don't like in the morning."

"Go pluck yourself," Chico said.

He had the telephone call transferred to the phone booth. It was Mrs. Collins.

"Mr. Tracy, the police have found Thomas. He's dead."

"Don't mention my name to them," Trace said.

"What?" she said.

"Never mind. I'm sorry about your husband."

"Thank you. They called last night. Oh, Mr. Tracy, he was murdered, they said."

"I'm sorry I wasn't able to find him earlier," Trace said. "Do the police have any idea who did it?"

"They didn't say," Judith Collins said.

"Well, I'm really sorry."

"The police want to talk to you."

"What? Why me?"

"I mentioned to them last night that you were looking for Thomas. They want to talk to you."

"I'm leaving San Francisco real soon. I don't have time to talk to them."

"I really think they want to talk to you, Mr. Tracy," she said ominously.

"This is what happens when you try to do somebody a favor," Trace whined. "Why didn't they call me themselves if they want to talk to me?"

"I told them I'd speak to you this morning. I guess if you don't go to see them, then they'll send someone to interview you."

Trace talked to the woman for a few more minutes, then hung up. When he stepped out of the phone booth, Chico, who had been eavesdropping, said, "Slowly the net is tightening around you, you accomplice after the fact.

You should have called the police when I told you to."

"Another thing I don't like in the morning is I-told-you-so," he said.

Following Judith Collins' directions, they found the sheriff's office near the town of Nicasio. Trace saw Mrs. Collins' beat-up old Plymouth Duster parked outside the building and pulled in alongside it.

Inside the door was an enormously fat policeman with a nametag reading COLES pinned to his pocket. He was very bald and his forehead wrinkled as he looked at them questioningly.

"I understand you found the body of a Thomas Collins. I'm Devlin Tracy with the Garrison Fidelity Insurance Company. We have a policy on the deceased."

The officer nodded and looked at Chico.

"I'm just along for the ride," Chico said. "I used to be a friend of his," she said, pointing to Trace.

"You know, little lady, I met a girl once in Korea during the war. Beautiful little thing. Could have been your twin."

"She's not Korean," Trace said.

"Her name was Chang Shi," the officer said.

"No relation," Trace said.

"Is your name Chang too?" the policeman asked Chico.

"No. It's Mangini. Michiko Mangini."

"Would you mind if I called you Chang Shi?"

"Of course not. Would you mind if I called you Telly Savalas?" she said.

The smile on the fat police officer's face vanished. Suddenly he was all business.

"You'll want to talk to Dick Carey. He's the deputy handling the case. In the back," he said without warmth, jerking his finger over his shoulder.

The door to the office of Deputy Sheriff Carey was open and Trace saw Mrs. Collins sitting in a chair, facing the officer, who was a tall man with a creased, weather-burned face and thick black hair. He saw Trace in the doorway and said, "Can I help you, sir?"

"Name's Tracy, Sheriff."

Judith Collins turned around. "That's Mr. Tracy from the insurance company. I told you about him."

"All right," he said pleasantly. "Come on in, Tracy."

"This is my friend Miss Mangini," Trace said.

"Sit down, both of you," Carey said.

"It was really Thomas," Judith Collins told Trace. "They took me to the morgue and it was really Thomas. He's dead."

"I'm really sorry," Trace said.

"Who would kill Thomas like that?" his wife asked. "He didn't have an enemy in the world."

Trace and Chico exchanged glances. If ever a man didn't fit that description, it was Thomas Collins.

Sheriff Carey saw the glance and folded his arms in front of him.

"There was a Little League baseball bat found nearby. The blood on it matches Collins'," he said.

"Fingerprints?" Trace asked.

Carey shook his head. "You don't mind my asking, Mr. Tracy, but just what have you been doing here?"

"Mrs. Collins asked me to look for her husband. I was trying to find him. Did you find his car?"

"They didn't find his car," Judith Collins said. "Now, why wasn't his car at the farm?"

Trace looked at Carey, but the policeman was impassive.

Suddenly Judith Collins began to weep. Tears streamed down her face. Her shoulders heaved.

Chico went and put her arm around the woman and looked at the deputy sheriff.

"I'm done with Mrs. Collins," he said apologetically.

"I'll take her outside, then," Chico said. "Trace, I'll wait for you."

Trace nodded, and as the two women left the room, Carey asked him, "Is it customary for an insurance detective like you to be involved in something like this?"

"I was looking for Collins as a favor for a friend. I didn't know him or his wife before," Trace said.

"The body's been lying around for a week.

Maybe you should find some other line of work."

"How'd you find the body?" Trace said, trying to ignore the insult. He reached into his pocket for his pack of cigarettes. His hand touched the diamond necklace that he had found in Collins' hand.

"A little farm near here. Somebody was driving by and the barn door was open. He looked in, saw the body, and called us."

"When was that?"

"Last evening," Carey said.

"Who was driving by and saw the barn door open?"

"Anonymous. Called us with the tip and hung up. Didn't give a name. What did you find out in your week of looking around?"

Trace took a deep breath. It was now or never, and Deputy Sheriff Carey seemed like a nice reasonable sort of guy for a policeman.

"I found the body three days ago," Trace finally said.

Carey's eyebrows raised in what Trace hoped was pleasant surprise.

"The farm belonged to Collins. Did you know that?" Trace asked.

Carey nodded. "Real-estate records show it. Tell me about finding the body."

"And this too," Trace said. He reached into his pocket and put the diamond necklace on the desk. "It was on the body."

Carey looked at it for a long time and said,

"You've been very busy, Mr. Tracy. Why don't you tell me all about it?"

Trace did. All of it, from beginning to end. The only thing he left out was that Chico had been with him at the farm. When he was done, he took another deep breath and sat back in his chair. It felt good to purge the soul.

Carey was nodding and smiling. "Tell me, Mr. Tracy, why did you do all these things?"

"I wanted to make sure some killer didn't get away," Trace said.

"It might have helped if you had given us this information and this necklace sooner," Carey said mildly.

"I was going to, but I had a dinner to go to."

"A dinner?"

"In San Francisco. At a convention. I was the guest of honor. I'm a war hero."

"Mr. Tracy, I'm mightily impressed. So much so that I want you to be the guest of honor around here for a while too." His voice suddenly turned ice-cold. "Stand up, please."

Trace did, and Carey came around the desk. "Please put your hands behind you."

When Trace complied, Carey put handcuffs on them, then patted Trace down, looking for a weapon.

"What are you doing?" Trace said.

"I'm arresting you."

"I thought we were both reasonable men," Trace said.

"No. I'm a reasonable man. At the very least you're a sneak thief and maybe even a murderer."

"I was only trying to help," Trace said. "Come on. You can't be serious."

"I'm a very serious man, Mr. Tracy. Serious *and* reasonable," the deputy sheriff said. "I've got high blood pressure and I'm very careful to keep my bad temper in check so I don't have a stroke. Otherwise, I'd just twist your fucking head off your fucking neck." He was starting to shout. "Trying to help? I need your fucking help like I need fucking hemorrhoids."

"Watch the blood pressure," Trace said.

"Trace, are you almost done? Oooops." It was Chico's voice.

Trace turned and saw her in the doorway. He shook his head imperceptibly, cautioning her to silence.

"What's going on?" she said.

"I'm booking your friend for obstruction of justice," Carey said.

"For what?"

"For withholding evidence. He found the body and he found a necklace and he never reported either."

"How do you know he did that?" Chico asked.

"He just told me," Carey said.

"Doesn't that sound like reporting it to the police? It does to me," Chico said.

"That's a wonderful point," Carey said. His voice was again calm and under control. "I'm sure it will make a great impression on the jury during his trial." He bellowed into the intercom, "Coles, get in here."

The fat balding officer arrived and Carey said, "Escort our friend here to a cell. He's staying with us awhile."

"And Chang Shi?" the bald officer said, nodding to Chico.

"Is that your name? Chang Shi?" Carey asked her.

Chico shook her head.

"She's free to go," Carey said. "Just put him in a cell."

As Trace was being led to the door, he started babbling to Chico. "Quick. Get Melvin Belli. Roy Cohn. William Kunstler. I'm sure some of my rights were violated. Call Swenson. Call my father. See if there's a parish priest around. I'll take a rabbi. Get me out of here. I'm innocent, I tell you. Innocent."

"Trace, you always overact," Chico said. "Underplay. Underplay. Dustin Hoffman, not Al Pacino."

"I don't want a review, I want a reprieve," Trace said.

"Come along you," Coles said, and led Trace by the arm out the office door.

"I'm allowed a phone call," Trace said.

"Who do you want to call?" Carey asked.

"Amnesty International," Trace said. "Chico, get right on it."

Then he was on his way down a long flight of stairs.

At the bottom, the bald officer unlocked a heavy fire door with a key from a ring on his belt. He pushed Trace through and down a narrow corridor. There were four cells on each side of the corridor, stark cells with thick iron bars and little cots with scrawny brown blankets thrown over them.

"You have a preference?" Coles asked. "Any one of the eight is yours."

"You have one with a view? Of Puerto Rico?" Trace said.

"Afraid not," Coles said. "This one will do." He put Trace in the last cell on the left. "You're our first criminal today," he said.

When the heavy cell door closed behind him and was locked with a key by Coles, Trace suddenly decided that this was serious business. He had been arrested and now he was in jail. Charged with a felony.

He immediately started planning his defense. He hadn't been read his rights. He hadn't been permitted a phone call. Coles had grabbed him by the arm, bringing him down the stairs. Maybe he could bump against the wall and bring up some bruises.

It wasn't much, but it was a start. False imprisonment, violation of his constitutional rights against self-incrimination, brutality, not being allowed to speak to counsel.

It was a snap. Even he could handle the defense. He was going to waltz out of this joint and then slap them with a fifty-million-dollar lawsuit.

Or else he was going to be convicted and sent up to the big house.

Is this the way it was going to end? Making license plates?

Maybe he could write a book about his experiences. He started to pace the cell as research for the book. It was four big paces in one direction and two and a half big paces in another direction. It'd be hard to call his imprisonment inhumane. His cell was bigger than the bedroom in most apartments he had lived in.

Look on the dark side, he told himself. Think in terms of movie rights.

Would he ever hear a bird sing? Would he ever see his children again? See? he told himself. Even prison has its good points.

This was getting him nowhere. He'd already been in jail five minutes and he still didn't have a theme for the book on his experiences. How was he going to get himself in the right morbid spirit?

Maybe if he had a drink.

Suddenly the whole crushing oppression of prison and the bleakness of his future pressed down on him, almost physically forcing the air from his lungs. He might never have another drink.

He felt like crying.

He ran to the cell door and wrapped his hands around the big bars. Just as he was about to start shouting for his freedom, he heard the door at the end of the corridor open.

He moved quickly to the corner of the cell, craned his neck, and saw Chico coming toward the cell, along with Coles.

"You got a visitor, Tracy," Coles said.

"Thank God. I was going crazy in stir," Trace said.

"Oh, will you stop it?" Chico said, standing in front of the cell. "You've only been in here two minutes."

"An eternity, baby, when you're a man without hope," Trace snarled from the corner of his mouth.

Coles unlocked the door. "You're free to leave," he said.

Trace cringed in a corner of the cell as the door opened. "This is a trick, isn't it? I'm going to walk away and you're going to shoot me in the back and say I was trying to escape."

"Get out of here before I shoot you where you stand," Coles said disgustedly. He turned to Chico and said, "Lady, you ought to get rid of this one before he drags you down with him."

"I know," Chico said. "I know."

Trace refused to talk until they were in the car and several blocks away from the sheriff's office.

Finally, he said, "Okay, what happened?"

"I convinced the sheriff that you were harmless," Chico said.

"So he dropped the charge?"

"He made it disorderly conduct. You're out on bail."

"How much bail?" Trace said.

"Fifty dollars," Chico said.

"Well, that's more like it," Trace said. After a while, he said, "Do I owe you fifty dollars?"

"You'll have to wait till my MasterCard bill comes."

"You bailed me out on plastic?" Trace said.

"Hey, baby, this is California," Chico said. "It's not all that easy, though."

"No. What's the catch?"

"I told Carey that we'd find out who the killer was before we left Frisco."

"And if we don't?"

"You may recapture the title of suspect number one," Chico said.

Trace pulled to the side of the road, stopped, and took the young Eurasian's hands in his. "Chico," he said earnestly.

"Yes?"

"Find that killer."

Tammy opened the door to the apartment above the gymnasium. When she saw Trace and Chico, she called out: "Julio."

Trace said, "We don't need him. I thought we'd talk in English."

"Try this. It's even better. We're not going to talk at all."

She started to close the door but Trace put his hand against it.

"Not even about blackmail?" he said. He

tried to breathe through his mouth. The temperature in the hallway was stifling and the air stale.

The young woman stopped pushing against the door. She was wearing a dirty bathrobe, even though it was mid-afternoon. Her hair was tousled about her head and Trace got the feeling that he had awakened her. Which led to a question. Didn't college students ever attend class anymore?

"What about blackmail?" Tammy said.

"I just heard an interesting story about your stepfather. Since it concerns you I thought you might want to comment on it before I tell it to the cops."

Julio stepped out of the back room. He was wearing his tight swimming trunks and his leather belt. As he came forward toward the door, Trace could smell him. He added that to his small list of perceivable smells. Julio.

"Whatcha want?" Julio grumbled. He stared hard at Trace. Tammy raise a hand to silence the beast. "It's all right, Julio," she said. "Dick Tracy's going to tell us a story." She hadn't stopped staring into Trace's eyes. "Come in, I suppose."

"I think we'd rather stay in the hall," Trace said. "The air's better out here."

"All right. Then tell me about blackmail."

"Remember how you told me that Collins tried to rape you? I'm sorry—should we refer to him as the dear departed? Or will Collins do?"

"Collins will do fine. Yeah, he tried to rape me."

"That's not exactly the way he saw it."

"No?"

"He tried to rape you?" Julio said to Tammy. He looked around in confusion as if searching for something to bite.

"Forget it, Julio. He's dead already," she said.

"He's lucky," Julio said.

"Well, he might argue the matter," Trace said. He looked at Tammy again. "Anyway, Collins said that you . . . you sure you want Julio to hear this?"

"Go ahead, talk," Tammy said.

"Collins said that you seduced him."

"That's a laugh," Tammy said.

"What's it mean, seduce?" Julio said.

"Never mind, Julio," Tammy said.

"Yeah. Never mind, Julio," said Trace. "Collins said that you asked for it, that you wandered around the house half-naked."

"I might as well have. That bastard was always undressing me with his eyes anyway," Tammy snapped.

"Then when it happened, he said you tried to get him to invest some money in a business with you. He claimed you made him a proposition that was hard to turn down: it was either turn over the cash or else you'd tell your mother that you'd been raped."

"Somebody tell me—what's it mean, seduce?" Julio said.

"Never mind, Julio," Trace said.

"That's all a lie," Tammy said. "Tell me, did Collins tell that story to some woman?"

Trace hesitated, then nodded.

"Sure," Tammy said. "He was trying to make himself out the big lover. Even his own step-daughter couldn't resist him. Well, he was a lying bastard. It never happened."

"What about the investment in a business? I guess that would be your little sweat parlor here."

"Yeah. I asked him once if his company would be interested. He laughed at me. He said I could go out and trick for the money."

Finally, a word had been used that Julio understood. "You don't go tricking for no-body," he said righteously, then looked around, pleased with himself.

"Never mind, Julio," Trace said.

"That's right, Julio," said Tammy. She told Trace, "Collins said he had friends who would set me up as a 'pro.' Dear old step-dad even suggested that maybe he'd throw me a dollar or two once in a while himself."

"You really hated him, didn't you?"

"I shouldn't?" she asked.

"I don't know. I don't know which one of you is a liar."

"I'm not going to talk to you anymore," Tammy said. "I don't think I should."

"You know I'm going to have to tell this story to the police," Trace said.

"That's your business, I guess," she said.

Julio said, "You want I should throw him out?"

"I am out," Trace said. "See? I'm out in the hall."

"I think I throw you downstairs then, flat-foots."

"Trace, I think we ought to go," Chico said.

"You're lucky, Julio," Trace said. "She's getting me out of here just in time."

Back in the car, Trace said, "Well? What do you think?"

"I don't like her any more than I did the other day," Chico said.

"You think she's telling the truth?"

"I don't know. What about you? What do you think?"

"I hope the rainy season starts soon," Trace said.

"What are you talking about?" Chico asked.

"I think it's the only way we're going to get Julio into a shower," Trace said.

Back at the hotel, the clerk desk intercepted Trace. "A package arrived for you, Mr. Tracy."

"What now?" Trace said to Chico. "All I want is a drink to celebrate my narrow escape."

"Cheer up. Maybe you won the Reader's Digest sweepstakes."

"Try to minimize the pluckiness, Chico. I warned you already once today. Pluck wears thin." Trace took a manila envelope from the clerk. It bore no return address. "It's probably from the IRS," Trace said. "Some new scam of theirs."

Chico took the envelope from his hands and opened it. The envelope contained a photo.

"That was fast," she said. "It's from Anselmo at the Fontana. Look at it. I bet that's your sweet Mandy the hooker."

Trace took the photograph. It was a grainy reproduction of a television picture. The time and date were stamped in a corner. It showed Thomas Collins sitting at a blackjack table. Next to him was a woman wearing the diamond butterfly necklace.

"Mandy?" Chico said.

"Close but no cigar," Trace said.

"Who is it?"

"Laurie Anders. Collins' secretary."

25

When they arrived at the Collins-Rose agency, Laurie Anders was bent over, rifling through the middle drawer of her desk. When she saw Trace, she pushed the drawer shut quickly.

"Mr. Rose isn't in," she said, running her hand nervously through her hair. "His in-laws are visiting and—"

"That's all right," Trace interrupted. "You're the one we wanted to talk to. This is Miss Mangini, my assistant."

"Me?" Laurie's voice rose an octave. "What do you want to talk to me about?"

Chico stepped up to the desk and breathed deeply. "Your perfume, for one thing," she said. "I've always liked Evening in Byzantium."

Laurie's face fell. "Thomas is dead, isn't he?"

"Sure is," Trace said. "How'd you do it?"

"I didn't do it." Laurie looked frantically from Trace to Chico. "I didn't. You've got to believe me."

226

"Sure," Trace said coldly. "You've got such a wonderful track record for telling me the truth."

The young blond woman sobbed. Chico stepped forward to put an arm around her, but Trace shook his head, warning her away. Warmth wasn't the way to go. He'd rather freeze it out of her.

Finally, she took a deep breath and wiped her eyes with a Kleenex. "You know," she said, shaking her head, "I had a feeling something was wrong when we didn't hear from Thomas last week. He didn't come in and he didn't call. I thought something was wrong." She smiled ruefully. "And I knew whoever found that perfume bottle might think of me." She covered her face with her hands. "This is a nightmare," she groaned. "It's not real. Things like this don't happen to people."

"They do when people commit murder," Trace said.

"But I didn't murder anybody," she snapped. "Maybe it looks that way, but I swear I didn't do it."

"Hold it," Trace said. "All this noise isn't helping. Maybe you should start at the beginning."

"How I started to work here?"

Trace took the photograph from the envelope and held it in front of her. "Like how you were at the Fontana Hotel with Thomas Collins. Maybe the truth this time?"

She gasped, staring at the picture, defeated.

"I was scared. I didn't know what was going on and I was afraid to tell you the truth." Her voice was small and very weak.

"Just because he was missing? That doesn't really hold a lot of water. How'd you wind up in Vegas with Collins? I thought you despised him."

"It was two weeks ago. He made me go."

"Tied your wrists and ankles with rope and dragged you into his car?" Trace said.

"No. He made me."

"It couldn't have been too bad," Trace said. "He bought you that diamond necklace, didn't he?"

"He did that almost as soon as we got to the hotel. Then he wanted it back two nights later."

"But you didn't give it to him," Trace said.

"No. He was losing so much money by then, I was afraid he wouldn't even have money left to buy gas to come home. He'd already borrowed all the money I brought with me."

"Did you argue?" Trace said.

She nodded. The tears started from her eyes again. "I told him I never wanted anything to do with him again. He laughed, the bastard. He said I'd do whatever he wanted, whenever he wanted, because I was already involved."

"Involved? Involved in what?" Trace asked.

She clenched her fists. "This is getting worse," she said.

"There aren't too many crimes worse than murder," Trace said.

Laurie's lips were set in a tight thin line. "I think maybe I've said enough."

Chico said, "We're easier than the police are going to be. Maybe I can help you. Collins was stealing money from the firm, wasn't he?"

Laurie's head snapped toward Chico in surprise. "How did you know?"

Chico shrugged. "He dropped a lot of cash at the Fontana, didn't he?"

"It was company money." Her eyes squinted and she looked pained. "I didn't have anything to do with it."

"I believe that," Chico said. "Tell us what happened. Maybe we can help."

"All right," she said, her voice almost a whisper. "Collins had set up a half-dozen phony firms. He was having company checks made out to them, as if they were legitimate contractors. Then he was cashing the checks and spending the money."

"How'd it involve you?" Trace asked.

"He was signing my name on the checks. I write most of the checks around here and he was signing my name. He was proud of how well he could forge it. He told me he practiced it thousands of times at home."

"How'd you find this out?" Trace asked.

"What I told you first was true, Mr. Tracy. I was at the farm once with him, about a year ago, and then I stayed away from him. He was after me, but I wouldn't go near him with a ten-foot pole. About a month ago, Mr. Rose was talking to me and he said the company was in a little trouble; our expenses were too high. He wanted me to do an analysis of spending, item by item. I went through the books and discovered all these companies that we were paying off: companies I'd never heard of. When I got out the checks, I saw my name on them but I didn't remember writing any of them."

"What happened then?" Chico asked gently.

"Mr. Rose was out, but Collins was in, so I went into his office to talk about it. I told him that I thought the checks were forgeries, and he closed the office door and said to me, that bastard, he said, 'Laurie, it looks like you're in a lot of trouble.' Then he started to laugh and said he didn't think I'd look good in prison stripes."

She looked up at Chico first, then Trace, searching their faces for sympathy.

Chico's face was impassive. Trace said, "How'd you find out it was Collins doing it?"

"He had me shaken up. And then he told me he was going to tell me something real confidential. He told me that he was pretty sure Mr. Rose was stealing money from the firm, but we couldn't say anything and we had to wait awhile. I didn't know what to do. I didn't really believe it, but I couldn't disbelieve it, either. Not in my situation."

"That was a month ago?" Trace asked.

She nodded, and Trace said, "So how'd you get to Vegas with him two weeks ago?"

"He told me he had an investigator working on the case and that we had to meet him in Las Vegas. We drove out, and once we got there, he bought me the necklace. I didn't know what it was all about until he told me, after a few too many, that he had been taking the money and forging my name and now we were partners. I don't know, Mr. Tracy. He filled my head with all kinds of things. I was scared to death. I was scared of jail and scared to run." She lowered her eyes. "I was even scared not to put out. I hated that bastard."

She was interrupted by someone coming in the office door. It was a young man and woman with a little boy in tow.

"We're looking for a house," the man said.

"We don't have one in here," Trace said.

"I mean, to buy a house. We want to buy a house."

Trace grabbed a handful of housing leaflets from the desk next to Laurie's and handed them to the man.

"Here, take these home and look through them. We've just had a death in the family and we're closing for the day. Come back next week."

"Oh," the man said, "I'm sorry."

"Quite all right," Trace said. "Nobody cared much for the deceased anyway."

After the family left, Trace locked the door, pulled the shade, and turned back to Laurie. "Now, you were saying."

"I didn't know what to do. For a couple of days, I just let it be. Then I talked to Collins

on the phone and told him I was going to tell
Mr. Rose. He told me not to. He had a plan to
straighten everything out, to return the money
and to get me off the hook so no one would
ever think I was involved. He said just being
involved might mean I'd never get my law
license. He convinced me to meet him that
night."

"And he took you to the farm?"

"Right," she said.

"When was that?"

"Tuesday a week ago," Laurie said. "We
drove up there in his car. He said he'd explain
everything to me when we got to the farm.
But when we got up there, all he wanted to do
was go to bed with me. He dragged me into
the bedroom. I screamed my head off, but
there wasn't anybody to hear me—Collins just
laughed and said I was the dumbest cunt in
three counties."

"What happened then?" Chico asked.

"I pushed him onto the bed to get away
from him. Then I grabbed the only thing I
could find in my purse, the perfume bottle,
and I threw it at him. It missed, but it gave
me a chance and I ran outside. It was raining
hard. His keys were still in the car, so I drove
away and left him there."

"What did you do with the car?"

"I didn't know what to do, so I put it in a
parking garage near here. It's still there, I
guess."

"You've got a parking stub?" Trace asked.

"Yes," Laurie said. She took it from her purse. "Right here."

Trace took it. "So that was the last time you saw Collins?"

Laurie nodded. "I swear. And he was alive when I left him. You've got to believe me."

"There are still a lot of questions to be answered," Trace said.

Laurie looked at him with a blank expression.

"The necklace," Trace said. "What'd you do with it?"

"I brought it to the office and put it in my desk. I was going to give it back to him, but I forgot about it. Then the other day when you were in here, I looked for it, but it was gone."

"You just left a diamond necklace in a desk drawer?" Trace said.

"The drawer is always locked. Our checkbook's in there."

"So somebody unlocked your desk and stole it," Trace said.

"I didn't take it out, but it's not there anymore," Laurie said. "Somebody must have stolen it."

"Who has the key to your desk?" Chico asked.

"There's only one key." She pointed behind her toward a bulletin board on the wall. "That's where I keep it, hanging on that hook."

Her face was downcast and miserable.

"There's something else, isn't there?" Chico asked.

"There's this. I just was getting out my

checkbook to write some checks and I opened the desk and found this."

She handed Trace a small black leather address book.

"The little black book," Trace said. He opened it to the Ms. The page was empty. Under *R*, he found written Mandy Reese's name. In capital letters. With a star next to it and the number "300." Mandy's price.

"Am I in trouble, Mr. Tracy?"

"Well, your diamond necklace was found on Collins' dead body. You had the car he was driving when he vanished. Your name is on a lot of illegal cash withdrawals from the company, your perfume is all over the dead man's bedroom drapes, and you hated the man. I think the cops'll say that's a start. Hell, they threw me in jail on less."

"That's 'cause you have a guilty look," Chico snapped. She patted Laurie Anders' shoulder. "Don't worry," Chico said. "You'll be all right. I have a good feeling."

26

"Good feeling about what?"

They hadn't heard the door open, and Rafe Rose stood there, staring at Laurie Anders' tear-soaked face. "What's going on here?"

"I didn't kill Mr. Collins," Laurie sobbed. "I swear I didn't."

Rose turned to Trace. "He's dead?"

"As Donny Osmond on Broadway."

"And you're acusing Laurie?"

"I'm not accusing anybody. I'm just looking for information."

"Well, you can stop badgering her," Rose snapped. "Laurie wouldn't hurt a fly."

"Somebody swatted Collins. How about you?"

Rose sputtered.

"When did you find out that Collins was stealing money from the company?" Trace asked.

There was a long silence.

Trace said, "You're going to have to tell

.t to the cops anyway, but telling me first might make the whole thing easier. Like a rehearsal."

"I had my suspicions," Rose said at last. "Then I found a lot of checks made out to phantom companies with postal boxes. The postal boxes were Thomas'. I have a friend in the post office who found out for me."

"My name was on the checks," Laurie sniffed.

"I knew you didn't have anything to do with it," Rose said. "I figured Thomas was signing your name. That's right, isn't it?"

Laurie numbly nodded.

"Did you confront Collins with this?" Trace asked.

"I was going to as soon as he came into the office. But he wasn't around to talk to. Then he turned up missing, and I didn't know what the hell was going on."

"You didn't just go up to his farm and beat his head in with a bat?" Trace asked.

"What farm?" Rose asked. "No, of course I didn't beat in his head with a bat."

"I'm going to report everything that happened today to the police," Trace said. "I'm sure they'll be in touch with you, so don't anybody leave town."

"Idiotic," Rose snapped. "Of course we're not leaving town."

"Where would I go?" Laurie said, and sounded miserable all over again.

*   *   *

Back at the Chinatown hotel, Trace sat Chico in the chair in his room and placed his tape recorder and all the tapes in front of her.

"What's this all for?" she said.

"I want you to sit down and play all these tapes again. Send out for room service. Don't leave. Listen and think."

"Oh. All of a sudden, I'm allowed to listen to your tapes. Every time I go near one of them you bitch, but now I can listen."

"This is serious business, Chico. I'm the one in the trouble. I'm out on bail, and if we don't find a killer pretty soon, I may go up the river."

"Uh-huh. And without a paddle." Chico scanned the room-service menu. She looked up and smirked. "So you want me to solve the case for you. After you've mucked it up for a week."

"Yes," Trace said.

Chico smiled. "Okay," she said.

27

Trace came back to the room at eleven P.M.

Chico was sleeping on the bed.

He sat alongside her and touched her shoulder. Her eyes opened languidly and she smiled.

"Hi, Trace. I've got it," she said.

"So do I," he said. "Can we make it stick?"

"We'd better," Chico said. "I don't have any recipes for cakes with files in them."

28

A heavy rain was drenching the ground when Trace and Chico arrived at the farm the next morning. Deputy Sheriff Carey was waiting and he looked at Trace with even less enthusiasm than normal.

"If this hocus-pocus of yours doesn't work, you're going right back into jail."

Chico said, "He might be guilty of hocus, but his pocus is clear."

"I ought to lock him up right now anyway, just on general principles."

Laurie Anders' car came up the driveway, and even before she could step out, Mike Mabley's gray Lincoln pulled in behind her.

Looking confused and a little frightened, Laurie walked toward Trace. Meanwhile, Mabley got out of his car and offered his arm to Mrs. Collins, who was wearing a black dress and veil. She took a look at the house and visibly shuddered.

"Glad you could make it," Trace called out to Mabley and Mrs. Collins.

"It was rather unexpected. My car wouldn't start and I had to ask Mr. Mabley to bring me here. It was very kind of him."

"That was real nice of you, Mike," said Trace. "I'd like you both to meet Laurie Anders and Deputy Sheriff Carey."

"Yeah, yeah," Mabley said. "Good to meet you. Couldn't we all head indoors? It's raining cats and dogs out here."

"We won't take long," Trace said.

"You haven't been much help in this whole matter so far," Mabley said. "Getting us all wet now isn't much of an improvement."

"I'll get better," Trace promised. "Laurie here was Thomas' secretary. She's the person he gave the diamond necklace to. The necklace I found in Collins' hand after he was killed."

"You found?" Mrs. Collins said. "But the police said . . ."

"I found the body first," Trace said. "I just hadn't gotten around to notifying them yet. As I said, Collins bought the diamond necklace in Vegas for Laurie."

"I didn't know anything about any diamond necklace," Mrs. Collins said.

"And Laurie's signature is on a number of fraudulent checks written from the real-estate firm," Trace said.

Sheriff Carey stared at him with narrowed

eyes. "Are you telling us that this woman's a criminal?"

"I didn't do it," Laurie said. "I didn't do anything."

A third car pulled into the driveway and Rafe Rose got out and walked toward them.

"Who's he?" Carey asked.

"Rafe Rose. He was Collins' partner," Trace said.

"Hello, Judith," Rose said. "I was sorry to hear about Thomas. Terrible. Just terrible."

"Thank you, Rafe."

Rose turned to face Trace and the police officer. "So what are we all doing here?"

"I was just about to ask the same question," Carey said.

"Last one," Trace said. He pointed to the driveway, where another battered car turned in. Tammy Collins and her boyfriend, Julio, stepped out and walked toward them.

"This is Collins' daughter," Trace said. "The neckless wonder is her boyfriend, Julio. I suggest you don't stand downwind of him."

"You've got a lot of nerve, Dick Tracy, dragging us here," Tammy snapped at Trace.

"Be patient. You might enjoy it."

Julio looked skyward, as if wondering when the rain would stop. It rained harder.

"Can we get on with it?" Carey asked.

"Okay," Trace said. "I found Collins' body back there in the little storage shed. Along the way I found out a lot about him. He was a womanizer, a gambler, and an embezzler."

"That's not all he was," Tammy snapped.

"You're right," Trace said. "He was a wife-beater too. And he even tried to snuggle up to sweet little Tammy here. To make a long eulogy short, everybody wanted him dead. Finally somebody did everyone a big favor by bopping him with a baseball bat. Anyway, I found the body and locked it up. Then a day later when I came back, someone else had been here. The barn door was open and there was a diamond necklace in Collins' hand. I couldn't have missed seeing that the first day."

"How'd it get there?" Carey said.

"Somebody planted it there. To incriminate Laurie."

Mike Mabley looked disgusted. "This is like something out of a movie," he said. "We're standing around in the rain listening to all this hooey and who knows if it makes any sense. Tracy, you were working on this case and didn't find out anything. If you had found Collins sooner, maybe he wouldn't be dead."

"That was one of the things," Trace said, "that was interesting. When I started to look for Collins, I didn't come up with anything. So suddenly Mrs. Collins gets a note that sends me on a search for some hooker. When that doesn't turn up anything, Mike happens onto a story in the paper that suggests that Collins and Rose had some money trouble. It was like the heat was always being turned up, trying to get something cooking."

"Are we leading somewhere?" Rose asked.

"We are. Stay with me," Trace said. "First thing was when I found out about this farm from Laurie . . ."

Mrs. Collins spun toward the young woman angrily. "Easy, Judith," Trace said. "Thomas is dead now. Anyway, when I was tipped off about the farm I found the body. I also found this sex newspaper with Mandy Reese's name and phone number circled. But Mandy told me that Collins had been her customer for a couple of years and that he had her phone number in a little black book. And she was listed in the telephone directory. So why would that ad be circled in the paper?"

"So that somebody would go looking for Mandy as a possible suspect," Chico said.

"Remember, Mrs. Collins had already gotten that note supposedly from Mandy, returning Collins' cuff link," Trace said.

"A printed note," Chico said. "But why would Mandy print a note? Why not just write it?"

"Because Mandy didn't send it," Trace said. "Someone else did, and they printed the message so that their handwriting wouldn't be recognized."

"The little black book was a mystery in itself," Trace said. "Mandy told me that Collins kept it in his wallet. But when I found his body, his wallet was still in his pocket. No little black book, though. It turned up yesterday in Laurie Anders' desk."

"Why?" Carey asked. "Who?"

"Because somebody was trying to throw suspicion all around. First on Mandy. And then, by putting the necklace in Collins' hands and planting the black book in her desk, on Laurie. Somebody who knew where the key was to Laurie's desk was kept. Somebody who killed Collins and took the little black book out of his wallet," Trace said.

"Don't forget the perfume bottle," Chico said.

"Right. When Laurie was up here just before Collins was killed, she threw a perfume bottle at him. I smelled the perfume in the bedroom and found a few little glass chips on the floor."

"The rest of the broken bottle was in the garbage pail," Chico said. "But if Laurie had killed him, she would have cleaned up the glass and disposed of it elsewhere. And the real killer would have just left it to throw suspicion on whoever the perfume belonged to."

"I'm totally confused now," Carey said.

"You're not the only one," Mabley said. "This is all just a big waste of time."

"I don't think so," Trace said. Rain was pouring down inside the collar of his jacket. He moved his foot through the soil of the yard, changing it into a red muddy paste.

"I picked up Collins car last night. It's coated with this red mud. It was raining here the last night Laurie saw Collins, the night he was killed."

"So?" Mabley said. "Mud's mud."

"I don't know," Trace said. "Red mud's pretty distinctive. Like the kind I saw on your galoshes the first day I met you. Remember? You told me you had to change a tire in the rain. But your car's brand-new and new tires just don't go flat that way."

"Are you hinting at something?" Mabley said.

"More than that," Trace said. "Mrs. Collins, how'd you and your husband come to get an insurance policy from Mabley? I mean, he's in San Francisco and you live out over the bridge. Were you two just wandering around the Mission District slums one day and decided to stop into Mabley's office?"

"I don't know," Mrs. Collins said. "Thomas decided to go to Mr. Mabley. I don't know why he chose him."

"And then the two of you went there and signed the policy application, right in Mabley's office?"

"That's right," Mrs. Collins answered. "What's wrong with that?"

"Nothing, if your miraculous husband had a talent for being in two places at one time."

"Tracy, you're talking through your ass," Mabley said, "and we're not putting up with any more of it."

"We? Already it's we? Come on," Trace said.

"Why don't you lighten up and tell the sheriff how you both killed Collins? Confession's good for the soul."

"Bullshit," Tammy Collins hissed. "My mother wouldn't have the guts to kill that bastard."

"Look at her again and tell me that," Trace said. "A husband who beat her. A husband who sexually assaulted her daughter. A husband so cheap he wouldn't buy furniture for the house or pay for the daughter's tuition, but was going through the middle-aged crazies, I guess, and stealing from his company and spending it all on other women."

Trace turned to face Judith Collins. "Last night I went to the restaurant near Mabley's office, the same restaurant where you saw me, Mabley." Trace nodded toward the sodden agent. "It might interest Mrs. Collins to know that Mabley takes all his women there. Isn't that right, Mike?" No response. "But the waitresses there remember him being there most recently with *you*, Mrs. Collins. They describe you to a T. You're a frequent customer there with your insurance man, aren't you?"

"Don't answer any more questions, Judith," Mabley said. "Mr. and Mrs. Collins came to my office to sign that policy in my presence. I'll swear to that in court."

"Of course you would," Trace said. "You'd swear that you and Mrs. Collins weren't having an affair too, wouldn't you?"

"Ahhh, to hell with this," Mabley said.

"Don't worry, Mike," Trace said. "It'll be real easy for the police to find out whether any of your car tires has ever had a flat. And that person who called the sheriff's office reporting the body in the barn—that's on tape. I don't think it'll be too difficult for a voice analyzer to match it to your voice."

"You're crazy. I don't know what you're talking about. Hell, I only met Collins once."

"That's true. When you came here with Mrs. Collins to bash in her husband's head. You and Judith took care of that policy all by yourselves well before that. But I think the mud on the galoshes will prove you've been here before."

"You dirty . . ." Mabley lunged at Trace but stopped as Deputy Sheriff Carey pulled his pistol from his holster.

"Hold on, Mr. Mabley. Let's just take a look at those galoshes," he said.

The group walked to the gray Lincoln and Mabley opened the trunk. The galoshes were there, clean as the day they came from the factory.

Carey looked at Trace, who shrugged. "Sometimes people wash the mud off their galoshes. There'll be traces of the red mud on them anyway, or in the car."

"A lot of theories," Carey said. "But I don't see anything that'll stand up." He holstered his gun again.

"One last thing," Chico said. "And it'll stand up."

"What's that?"

Chico pulled a sheaf of papers from her big handbag. "Take a look at the insurance policy. Beneath the signatures."

"The date," Carey said.

"Right. The date. And that's the same date that Thomas Collins was in Las Vegas with Laurie Anders. And here's the proof." She pulled out the still shot of Collins and Laurie taken at the Fontana Hotel casino by the overhead security cameras.

"This picture was taken from a casino videotape," Chico said. "See the date and time are on the photo. They're right from the TV tape. Collins couldn't be in Mabley's office and in the casino at the same time."

She turned and smiled at Mabley.

Mrs. Collins began to weep.

"I think we had better all go to headquarters," Carey said. "And I think I should warn you two," he said to Mabley and Mrs. Collins, "that anything you say may be used against you. You have a right—"

"They have a right to get out of here," Tammy Collins said. "My mother's not going anywhere." She turned. "Julio, you know what to do."

Julio moved toward Carey. "I hate flatfoots," he said.

Trace tapped him on the shoulder, and when

Julio turned, Trace put a big fist into his face. The weight lifter fell over backward like a tree into the mud

"Not bad," Carey said.

"I hate people who mangle the English language," Trace said.

29

Three hours later, Trace came out of the sheriff's office and got into his car, where Chico was munching a hot dog.

"Where did you find food in the middle of this desert?" Trace asked.

"I saw a vendor driving by. I jumped out and flagged him down. What happened?"

"They admitted it finally," Trace said. "Mrs. Collins said that her husband was crazy and getting crazier. She suspected he was stealing money from the firm and that was okay with her. She was only in the marriage for the money anyway. But when he started flaunting all his other women in front of her she was afraid it was all going to vanish."

"How'd she meet Mabley?"

"That snotty kid told us about it when she mentioned that her mother belonged to some artisan's craft league. Mabley had a citation from that same outfit as a donor. They met there. The bat's from one of Mabley's Little League teams."

"They should have just killed Collins and had done with it and not jerked around with the insurance," Chico said.

"That was the mistake. They figured as long as they were going to kill him anyway they might as well get a few extra dollars out of it. It reminds me of something my father told me a long time ago."

"What was that?" Chico asked.

"Sarge said, 'Pigs get fat but hogs get slaughtered.' These two were hogs."

Trace chuckled as he drove off. "It must have driven them crazy, them expecting me to keep finding something, and me finding it but not telling them about it. They kept trying to throw suspicion on Mandy—and they didn't even know Mandy, she was just a name—or Laurie. They didn't care which. And they wanted me around as an alibi. 'Of course, Mrs. Collins had nothing to do with her husband's death. Didn't she ask Mr. Tracy to look into his disappearance?' Jerks."

Chico said, "I bet you're going to have one wonderful time calling Walter Marks and telling him about this, aren't you?"

"I don't know. I don't think I'll gloat. Groucho gave me my first clue."

"What was that?" Chico asked.

"When Mabley said that Groucho had told

him I was the best investigator in the insurance business. That's when I knew Mabley was a liar," Trace said.

When Trace came out of the shower, Chico walked through the connecting doors into his room.

"My mother's left," she said.

"Left? Left where?"

"She's gone to Hawaii. With Mr. Nishimoto. They just called from the airport. She sends you her love."

"And you wouldn't share a room with me," Trace said. "What are they doing in Hawaii?"

"Another convention. And Mr. Nishimoto's got a computer factory on Maui and a twenty-five-room house on his own beach."

"Sounds like your mother could make a career out of going to conventions," Trace said.

"Or seeing Mr. Nishimoto," Chico said.

"Yeah," Trace said. He looked out the window toward the street.

"What's the matter?" Chico asked.

"I was just thinking. I suppose you'd be happy with a Japanese zillionaire too, wouldn't you?"

"No way," Chico said. "Too short. I wouldn't feel right if I couldn't stare at a blond barbarian armpit while I was dancing."

Trace kissed her. "I'm a lucky man," he said.

"And a war hero too," Chico said.

"*Banzai*," he yelled, and scooped her up and carried her to the bed.

Thrilling Reading from SIGNET

		(0451)
☐	**THE EMERALD ILLUSION** by Ronald Bass.	(132386—$3.95)*
☐	**ON WINGS OF EAGLES** by Ken Follett.	(131517—$4.50)*
☐	**THE MAN FROM ST. PETERSBURG** by Ken Follett.	(124383—$3.95)*
☐	**EYE OF THE NEEDLE** by Ken Follett.	(124308—$3.95)*
☐	**TRIPLE** by Ken Follett.	(127900—$3.95)*
☐	**THE KEY TO REBECCA** by Ken Follett.	(127889—$3.95)*
☐	**TOLL FOR THE BRAVE** by Jack Higgins.	(132718—$2.95)†
☐	**EXOCET** by Jack Higgins.	(130448—$2.95)†
☐	**DARK SIDE OF THE STREET** by Jack Higgins.	(128613—$2.95)†
☐	**TOUCH THE DEVIL** by Jack Higgins.	(124685—$3.95)†
☐	**THE MIERNIK DOSSIER** by Charles McCarry.	(136527—$3.95)
☐	**THE SECRET LOVERS** by Charles McCarry.	(132432—$3.95)*
☐	**THE TEARS OF AUTUMN** by Charles McCarry.	(131282—$3.95)*
☐	**THE LAST SUPPER** by Charles McCarry.	(128575—$3.50)*
☐	**FAMILY TRADE** by James Carroll.	(123255—$3.95)*

*Prices slightly higher in Canada
†Not available in Canada

**Buy them at your local
bookstore or use coupon
on last page for ordering.**

Medical Thrillers from SIGNET

**Buy them at your local
bookstore or use coupon
on last page for ordering.**

Great Horror Fiction from SIGNET